Death Wish

Something unearthly and strange was happening to him. He was a flier, a test-pilot. He had known pressure before. But this was the speed of interstellar flight—and it was tearing at the separate cells of his flesh . . . pulling them apart.

Anguish became terror . . . terror turned into blind panic. His body was going to pieces.

Then he saw Shairn . . . the irresistible she-devil Varddan who had convinced him he was destined to fly the starways. What a mockery! He was going to die, and she had known it all along.

He was glad he could see her . . . glad that she looked so beautiful. Because pressure, or no pressure, he was going to live . . . just long enough to kill her!

BOOKS BY LEIGH BRACKETT
Published by Ballantine Books

THE BEST OF LEIGH BRACKETT

THE BOOK OF SKAITH
  Volume One: THE GINGER STAR
  Volume Two: THE HOUNDS OF SKAITH
  Volume Three: THE REAVERS OF SKAITH

THE LONG TOMORROW

THE STARMEN OF LLYRDIS

FOLLOW THE FREE WIND

THE STARMEN
OF LLYRDIS

Leigh Brackett

A DEL REY BOOK

BALLANTINE BOOKS • NEW YORK

A Del Rey Book
Published by Ballantine Books

ISBN 0-345-28483-6

Manufactured in the United States of America

First Edition: January 1976
Second Printing: November 1980

Cover art by Dean Ellis

THE STARMEN
OF LLYRDIS

I

MICHAEL TREHEARNE WAS TO REMEMBER THAT EVE-
ning as the end of the world, for him. The end of his familiar life in a familiar Earth, and the first glimmering
vision of the incredible. It began with the man who
spoke to him on the heights behind St. Malo, by the
light of the Midsummer Fires.

There was a great crowd of tourists there, come to
watch the old Breton festival of the sacred bonfire. Trehearne was among them, but not of them. He stood
alone. He was always alone. He was thinking that the
ritual being performed in the wide space of stony turf
was just too quaint to be endured and wondering why he
had bothered with it, when someone said to him with
casual intimacy,

"In four days we shall be through with all this, going
home. A good thought, isn't it?"

Trehearne turned his head, and looked into a face so
like his own that he was startled.

The resemblance was that of a strong racial stamp,
rather than any blood kinship. If two Mohawks were to
meet unexpectedly in the hills of Afghanistan they
would recognize each other, and it was the same with
Trehearne and the stranger. There was the same arrogant
bone-structure, the odd and striking beauty of form and
color that seemed to have no root in any race of Earth,
the long yellow eyes, slightly tilted and flecked with
sparks of greenish light. And there was the same pride.
In Trehearne it was a lonely, bitter thing. The stranger
bore his like a banner.

During the moment in which Trehearne stared,

1

amazed, the stranger remarked, "I don't remember seeing you on the last ship. How long have you been here?"

"Since yesterday," answered Trehearne, and knew as he formed the words that they were not the ones expected of him. A wild throb of excitement ran through him. He said impulsively, "Look here, you've mistaken me for someone else, but I'm glad you did!" In his eagerness he all but clutched the man's arm. "I must talk to you."

Something in the stranger's expression had altered. His eyes were now both wary and startled. "Upon what subject?"

"Your family—my family. Forgive me if I seem impertinent, but it's important to me. I've come a long way, from America to Cornwall and now to Brittany, trying to trace down my own line . . ." He paused, looking again into that remarkable face that watched him, darkly handsome, darkly mocking in the firelight. "Will you tell me your name?"

"Kerrel," said the man slowly. "I beg your pardon, Monsieur. The resemblance is indeed striking. I mistook you for one of my kin."

Trehearne was frowning. "Kerrel?" he repeated, and shook his head. "My people were called Cahusac, before they went into Cornwall."

"There was doubtless a connection," said Kerrel easily. He pointed abruptly to the open space beyond. "Look—they begin the final ritual."

The great bonfire had burned low. The peasants and the fisherfolk, some hundreds of them, were gathered in a circle around the windy glow of the flames. A white-bearded old man began to pray, in the craggy Breton Gaelic.

Trehearne barely turned his head. His mind was full of the stranger, and of all the things that had oppressed and worried and driven him since childhood, the nagging little mysteries about himself to which now, perhaps, he would find the key.

He glanced away only a second, following the gesture of Kerrel's arm. But when he looked back, Kerrel was gone.

Trehearne took half a dozen aimless steps, searching

2

for the man, but he had melted away into the darkness and the crowd, and Trehearne stopped, feeling sold and furious.

His temper, long the bane of a rather luckless existence, reared up and bared its claws. He had always been childishly sensitive to insults. If he could have got his hands on the contemptuous Kerrel he would have thrashed him. He turned again to the festival, controlling himself as he had learned painfully to do, realizing that he was being ridiculous. But his face, so like that of the vanished stranger, had a very ugly look around the mouth.

The Bretons had begun the procession around the waning fire. Short, burly men in bright jackets and broad-brimmed hats, sturdy women in aprons and long skirts, their improbable starched coifs fluttering with ribbons and lace. Sabots clumped heavily on the stony ground. They would march three times sunward, circling the embers, and then solemnly, each one, pick up a pebble and as solemnly cast it into the coals. Then they would scramble for the charred brands and bear them home to be charms against fever and lightning and the murrain until the next Midsummer Eve.

It struck Trehearne that most of them, except the very old, looked painfully self-conscious about it all. In a thoroughly bad humor, he was on the point of leaving. And then he saw the girl.

She was standing some ten feet away from him, in the forefront of the crowd, which had shaped itself into a semi-circle. She had wanted him to see her. She was swinging a white hand-bag like a lazy pendulum on a long strap, and her gaze was fixed on him. She was smiling, and the smile was an open challenge.

In the reflection of the great bed of glowing embers, Trehearne saw that she was another of Kerrel's breed —and his own, whatever it might be. But it was not that recognition that made his heart leap up. It was herself.

The red-gold light danced over her, and perhaps it was only that faery glow that made her seem more than a handsome girl in a white dress. Only a trick of wind and starlight, perhaps, that made Trehearne see in her a changeling, bright, beautiful, wicked, and wise, and no more human than Lilith.

3

She beckoned to him, with a small imperious movement of her head. He had forgotten his anger for the moment, but now it returned. He began to walk toward her, across the front of the crowd, a tall man, splendidly built and strong, bearing in his own face the stamp of that strange, wicked beauty, his eyes yellow as the fire and as hot. She saw that he was angry, and she laughed.

Whether it was the sound of her laughter that drew the attention of the Bretons, or merely a chance look, Trehearne never knew. He came up to her, and she said,

"I am a Kerrel, also. Will you talk to me?"

He was about to answer, when he realized that the noise of the sabots had broken rhythm, and that the crowd of tourists was staring at him and the girl and then past them at the Bretons. He heard an uneasy muttering of questions in French and English, and behind him a great silence.

He turned. The ritual circle was broken. The old man who had prayed was coming toward them, and with him were other men and women, drawn as though by some compulsion from the ranks of the marchers. They were all old, their faces weathered and seamed by the passing of many winters, and in their eyes he saw the spark of an ancient hatred, the shadow of an ancient fear.

He had seen that same look among the older country folk of Cornwall—directed at himself.

The old man raised his hand. He stopped only a few feet away, and the others with him. There was something infinitely threatening in the squat monolithic bulk of that little crowd, a survival from an older world. The girl flung up her head and laughed, but Trehearne did not feel like laughing.

The old man cursed them.

Trehearne had not one word of Gaelic, but he did not need a knowledge of the tongue. Nor did he need to have explained to him the gesture of angry dismissal. The Bretons had already picked up their brands from the fire. In another minute, they would use them, on himself and the girl.

He caught her rather roughly by the arm, but she pulled away and shouted something at the old man, still laughing, still mocking, and he thought again that she was a changeling and no ordinary girl. The words she

4

spoke might have been Gaelic, but they had a different sound. Whatever they were, they held no kindness. Trehearne thrust his way through the sightseers, who parted readily to let him through, and in a minute the girl came after him. The voice of the old man followed them down the slope of the hill, and the curious tourists stared after them until they were out of sight.

The girl said, "Are you still angry?"

"What's the matter with them?" demanded Trehearne.

"The peasant folks have long memories. They don't understand what it is they remember, only that evil things once happened to them, because of us."

"What sort of evil things?"

"Have there been any new ones since the beginning?" Her voice held a dry humor. Trehearne had to admit there hadn't been. From the stealing away of maidens to witchcraft, family legends tended to a wearying sameness.

"However," he added, "the Kerrels and the Cahusacs both must have been outstanding in their field, judging from the reception they gave us back there."

He stopped. They were far from the crowd now. The walled island city bulked huge and dark, a medieval shadow against the night and the sea. The girl was a white wraith in the gloom, all astir with the salt wind that tumbled her hair and set her skirts to rippling. He did not speak to her, but stood there silently, trying to see her face in the starlight. After a while she asked him,

"What is in your mind?"

"I am waiting to see if you will vanish like the other Kerrel."

She laughed. "Kerrel is a rude man. I have offered myself to make amends. Surely you can't be angry now!"

It was his turn to laugh. "No. In fact, I'm thankful for your—by the way, what relation is he to you?"

"None."

"But you said—"

"It was a small lie, and it served its purpose."

"Well, anyway, I'm thankful for Kerrel's rudeness. I'd much rather talk to you!" His ill-humor was quite gone.

He took her hand, and was amazed to find how strong it was. The girl seemed to radiate an immense vitality, an aliveness that made all the other women of his knowing appear like half-awakened clods.

"What do they call you," he asked, "who are *not* a Kerrel?"

"Shairn."

"That doesn't sound Breton."

"Doesn't it? My other name is even more unusual. It's unpronounceable, and means *of the Silver Tower.*"

Her eyes were very bright in the starshine. He thought that in some secret way she was mocking him, but he did not care. He said, "I'll stick to Shairn." They had started down the path again. He told her his own name, and she asked,

"You are American?"

"Fourth generation."

"From Brittany to Cornwall to America," she murmured, as though to herself. "The years, the generations, the mingling of other strains—and still the Vardda blood breeds true! Michael, you're wonderful!"

He repeated the word *Vardda,* wonderingly.

"A tribal name. You've never heard it." She laughed with pure delight. "You're incredible. No wonder Kerrel made a mistake! Listen, Michael. You wonder about your family, your race. Oh, yes, I heard all that. Well, perhaps I'll tell you—or again, perhaps I won't! There's a little cove beyond the lighthouse. I'll meet you there, in the morning."

II

MORNING IS AN INDETERMINATE TIME FOR AN APPOINTMENT. Trehearne made it early, clambering over the spray-wet rocks. The sun was warm, and the sea was very blue, flecked with white foam. A high excitement burned in him. He had not slept, thinking of the girl Shairn and the man Kerrel, trying to analyze the strangeness that clung about them and touched some buried chord within himself. He had not succeeded.

There was something almost fierce in the way he moved. He was oppressed by a fear that Shairn would not come. He felt that she was playing some game of her own with him, though for what purpose he could not guess. But having started the game, he was going to see to it that she played it out. If she did not come he would find her, if he had to take the stones of St. Malo apart to do it.

He found the cove. It was deserted. Reason told him that he was impatient, but he was disappointed and angry all the same. Then, looking closer, he saw footprints in the sand, small naked ones leading to the water. A beach robe and a pair of sandals were tucked into a crevice in the rocks.

He searched the waves that rolled idly in between two grey, tumbled shoulders. There was no sign of her. Trehearne's eyes took on a hard, bright glint. He stripped off his shirt and slacks and plunged into the cold surf.

He was an excellent swimmer. In his college days he had gone through a phase of being a star athlete, until he was stopped by a vague conviction that his physique had been designed for something more important than leaping over bars and running arbitrary distances on a cinder track. He had never found the important thing, but the conviction remained with him. It was part of that pride which was the mainspring of his character—a meaningless pride, he was forced to admit, which had served only to make trouble between himself and the world.

He made the circuit of the cove twice before he found her, hiding among the broken rocks of the north wall, half veiled in glistening weed, laughing at him. He reached for her and she went under him like a dolphin, breaking water ten feet away to splash and dive again.

He chased her down into the rustling blue-green depths and up again to the sunlight and the foam, and her body was the color of silver, fleet and lithe and wondrously strong. He might have caught her, but he did not, only touching her with his fingers to show her that

7

he could. Her hair was unbound, a streaming darkness around her head, and her mouth was red, and her eyes were two green dancing motes of the sea itself, unknowable, taunting, fickle as the waves.

At last she rolled over on her back to float, breathless, pleased with herself and him.

"Let us rest!" she said, and he floated near her, watching the motion of her white arms in the water. The lines of an old poem came unbidden to his tongue.

" 'What bright babes had Lilith and Adam—
'Shapes that coiled in the woods and waters,
'Radiant sons and glittering daughters . . .' "

"The man who wrote that knew only half the truth," said Shairn. "Let's go in."

They found a sheltered spot where the sun was warm. Absently, Shairn smoothed a patch of sand with her palm, and rumpled it again. After a while she said,

"What sort of a man are you, Michael? What do you do? How do you live?"

He looked at her keenly. "Do you really want to know? All right, I'll tell you. I'm a man who has never been satisfied. I've never had a job I could stay with very long. I'm a flier by trade, but even that seems a dull and rather childish business. And why? Because I'm too good for any of it."

He laughed, not without a certain cruel humor. "Don't ask me in what way I'm too good. I seem to be unusually healthy, but that's only important to me. My brain-power has never set the world on fire. I have no tendency to genius. In fact, a suspicion creeps upon me that I'm just not good enough. Whichever way it is, there has always been something lacking, either in me or the world."

Shairn nodded, and again he was conscious of a queer wisdom in her that did not fit with her youth. She smiled, a small thing full of secrets.

"And you thought that if you learned the origin of your blood you would understand yourself."

"Perhaps. My father was a weedy little man with red hair. He swore I was none of his. I didn't look like my

8

mother's side, either. I've never looked like anybody, until I met you and Kerrel. Oddness becomes very wearing, especially when you don't know why you should be odd." He added, "The villagers in Cornwall called me changeling. I had the same thought when I saw you."

"So we are of one race. Could you stay with me, Michael?"

"You're not a woman, you're a witch. I've never met a witch before."

She laughed outright at that. "Nonsense. Witch, changeling—those are words for fools and peasants."

"Who are the Vardda, Shairn?"

She shook her head. "I told you last night. It is a tribal name. You were saying to Kerrel that you had come to Brittany to trace down your family. Do you know where to start?"

"I learned in Cornwall that they came from a place called Keregnac."

He thought she started a little at that name, but she said nothing, and he asked, "Do you know the town?"

"It's not a town," she answered slowly. "Only a tiny village, lying on the edge of a great moor. Yes, I know Keregnac." She picked up a bit of driftwood and began to draw idle patterns in the sand. "I don't think you will learn much there. The village is very old, and is now almost dead."

"But," he said, "I don't have to worry about that now, do I?"

"How do you mean?"

"You, Shairn. You know about my family, my race. I don't have to depend on Keregnac. You'll tell me."

She flung down the bit of driftwood. "Will I?"

"You said last night—"

"I don't remember what I said. And anyway, one says many things at night that sound foolish in the daytime." She stood up. "Perhaps Kerrel was right."

"About what?"

"About you. He made quite a scene when I joined him again. He said a number of things, and some of them were true."

"Such as what?" asked Trehearne evenly.

"Such as that heredity has played a rather cruel trick

9

on you, and that you're better off to know nothing about your ancestry. Get me my robe, Michael, I must go."

But he had reached out and caught her wrist, and his grip was not gentle. "You can't do that," he said. "You can't refuse to tell me now."

"Oh," she said softly, "but I can. And I do."

"Listen," said Trehearne. "I've come a long way, and I've been through a lot. You're a beautiful woman, and I suppose you have a right to your whims, but not about this."

She looked down at his hand that was locked so tight around her wrist, and then up at him again, and her eyes were bright and very hot. "Is that your idea of persuasion?"

"Are you going to tell me?"

"No." She showed him her teeth, silently, in a catlike smile. "Kerrel is waiting for me."

"Let him wait."

"But he won't. We're leaving St. Malo today, and I assure you he won't go without me." He dropped her wrist.

"I'll follow you."

Her eyes were blazing. "That will be a long way."

"Brittany is not so large."

"Did I say I live in Brittany?" She caught up the robe and flung it around her shoulders, and then she said, "All right, Michael, follow me. I'd like that. Follow me as far as you can!"

She left him, going swiftly over the tumbled rocks. Trehearne watched her until she was out of sight, not moving from where he stood. After a long while his gaze was drawn to the sand and the patterns that Shairn had traced there. Amid the aimless, rambling lines a word stood out in large clear letters.

KEREGNAC.

III

A HIRED CAR DRIVER TOOK TREHEARNE, FOR AN EXOR-
bitant price, to Keregnac. On the first day they had
roads, and made excellent time. On the second the tiny
Fiat labored in agony along rutted cart tracks. The sea
was far behind them, and the driver complained incessantly of the mad desires of Americans. Why should
anyone wish to go to Keregnac, a place that even the
Bretons had forgotten?

Trehearne was in a strange and savage mood. The
sound of Shairn's name was in his ears, and all the
things that she had said and done went round and round
in his head, and the more he thought of them the more
he hated her, and the more he wanted her. And the
more he hated Kerrel, who had her, and who was part
of whatever secret life she lived. But Shairn and her affairs were only part of it. He had come close to the end
of his quest. He had almost grasped it, only to be denied
at the last by a woman's fickle impulse. He would not be
denied any longer. Shairn had started something that
could not be stopped, no matter where it led.

The driver lost his way among the ruts and the stony
hamlets. When he begged directions, the peasants regarded Trehearne in dour silence and could not be com-
pelled to answer. It was impossible even to learn whether others had gone this way before them.

Trehearne had foreseen this possibility. He had had
enough such difficulties in Cornwall. He had got a map
and directions in St. Malo, and he forced the luckless
driver on by dead reckoning. It was night before they
came wallowing into a muddy square half paved with

11

ancient stones and saw the lights of half a dozen dwellings clustered around it.

"Go there, to the largest house," said Trehearne. "Ask if this is Keregnac, and tell the master we'll pay well for lodging."

The driver, himself in a thoroughly foul humor by now, did as he was bid, and in a few moments Trehearne found himself in a three-room house of crumbling stone, the walls blackened with smoke and age. A meagre fire burned on the hearth, and two home-made candles furnished all the light.

It was enough to show Trehearne's face.

Oddly enough, the squat, hard-handed peasant who was master of the house showed neither fear nor hatred. Nor was he surpised. A certain slyness crept into his sullen expression, but that was all.

"You shall have the best bed, Monsieur," he said, in vile French and pointed to a gigantic carved *lit-clos*. "I have also one good horse. The others have gone ahead into the *landes*. You will wish to overtake them."

Trehearne tried to conceal his excitement. "Monsieur Kerrel and Mademoiselle Shairn?"

The peasant shrugged. "You know better than I what their names might be. I am not a curious man. I enjoy good health, and am content."

He called sharply in the Breton tongue, and a woman came to prepare food. She had a heavy, stupid face. She glanced once, sidelong, at Trehearne and after that was careful neither to look at nor speak to him. As soon as the simple meal was on the table, she hid herself in the adjoining room.

The ancient crone who sat knitting by the fire was not so cowed. As though age had placed her above necessity, she kept her bright little eyes fixed upon Trehearne with a mixture of hostility and interest.

"What are you thinking, *ma vielle?*" he asked her, smiling.

She answered, in French that was almost unintelligible to him, "I am thinking, Monsieur, that Keregnac is greatly honored by the Devil!"

The man snarled at her in Gaelic, bidding her be silent, but Trehearne shook his head.

"Don't be afraid, *grandmère*. Why do you say that?"

"From time to time he sends his sons and daughters to us. They eat our food, borrow our horses, and pay us well. Oh, very well! We could not live, if it were not for them."

Her white coif bobbed emphatically. "But it is still the devil's money!"

Trehearne laughed. "And do I appear like the devil's son?"

"You are the very breed."

Trehearne bent closer to her and said, "Once my family lived here. Their name was Cahusac."

"Cahusac," she said slowly, and between her gnarled fingers the clicking needles stopped. "Eh, that was long and long ago, and Keregnac has forgotten the Cahusacs. They were driven out . . ."

"Why?"

"They had an only child, a daughter, who married one of these handsome sons of the Evil One, and . . ." She paused and looked at him wisely. "But forgive me, my old tongue has not yet learned caution."

Trehearne dropped to one knee beside her, so that he might see her face more clearly. His heart was hammering. "No, no, *grandmère!* Don't stop—it was to hear these things that I came all the way from America. This daughter of the Cahusacs—she had a child?"

"And the villagers would have stoned her to death, and the babe too. But she knew, and fled away." She straightened up and her eyes had grown bleak and stern. "We take their silver, and that is sin enough. And I have spoken too much, and will speak no more."

"No, please!" Trehearne said. "Who are these strangers—these Vardda? You must know. You must tell me!"

But she sat like an image carved from dark wood, her head bent forward over the pale wool spread in her lap. Trehearne stood up, mastering a desire to shake her until the words came, and then he went outside. He walked the few paces to the end of the muddy street and looked out upon a moor that stretched still and desolate under the stars. He stood there for a long time, staring out across the empty heath, his eyes narrowed and intense with thought.

Into these wastes, the *landes*, Shairn had gone with

13

Kerrel. Why, for what purpose, he could not guess, any more than he could guess the answers to all the other riddles, and he knew better than to ask his host. The silence mocked him, full of secrets.

He had made some progress. He had traced his family back to Keregnac, and he knew now the reason for their leaving. A Vardda hybrid snatched from death at the hands of an irate peasantry—a romantic story, but unrevealing. The answer to the riddle of his birthright lay still farther on.

How much farther, he did not dream.

At dawn he paid off his driver and his host, mounted the horse that was ready for him, and struck out into the moor. He had no idea what direction he should take. However, the moor could not be endless in extent, and if he searched long enough he was almost bound to find what he was looking for. If Kerrel and Shairn and other "sons and daughters of the devil" came into the *landes*, they must have shelter of some kind.

But all that day he rode, across marshland and stony soil, through gorse and bramble and stunted trees, without seeing a cottage or a solitary sheep or even a distant smoke to mark a human habitation. Only here and there a lonely tor stood like a druid sentinel against a lowering sky.

It drew on to dusk. The wind blew, and it began to rain, a fine soaking drizzle that showed promise of going on all night. And still the heath stretched on all sides of him, featureless, without comfort or hope.

There was nothing to do but go on. He let the horse find its own way, sitting hunched in the saddle, wet and wolfishly hungry and at odds with the world.

His mood grew blacker as the light failed. The horse continued to plod on through pitch darkness. The land rolled a good bit, and Trehearne knew from the cant of the saddle when his mount slid down into the hollow of a fold and then scrambled out again up the other side, slipping and stumbling in the mud and wet gorse. It was from the crest of one such low rise that he caught a glimmer of light, and ahead and to the left.

He said aloud, "There is a cotter's hut," and would not allow himself to hope for anything else. But he spurred the horse on recklessly. Even so, it seemed hours before he reached the light.

He was close onto the place before he could make out its size and shape in the thick darkness. Then he reined in, completely baffled. This was no cotter's hut, nor was it a manor, nor any normal sort of dwelling. He saw a broken shaft of stone that had once been a squat crenellated tower, and around its foot was a ruin of walls and outbuildings. It was very old, Trehearne thought—probably medieval, and probably the onetime stronghold of a robber baron.

A ruin, lost in the wasteland. And yet it was inhabited. Yellow lamplight poured from the embrasures of the keep. There were horses in the courtyard. There was a sound of voices, and in the rickety outbuildings that leaned against the wall there were lanterns and noises and activity. Trehearne sat still for a time, trying to make some sort of sense out of what he saw, and failing. Then he dismounted and let his weary animal join its fellows, going himself toward the outbuildings and the men who were working there. He carried a small automatic in his pocket. He was not afraid, but he was glad he had it. There was an unsettling queerness about the place, about its situation and whatever reason it had for being.

The wooden structures were not nearly so tumbledown as they seemed at first look. In fact, Trehearne had a ridiculous idea that they had been built that way deliberately. They were crammed now with crates and packing cases, not wooden ones, Trehearne noticed, but light, strong plastic, marked with unfamiliar symbols. Others were being fetched up through openings in the stone that led apparently into the cellars beneath the keep. The men who handled them, with a good deal of laughter and loud talk, were mostly young, and all of the Vardda stock, and their dress was as strange as their language. Trehearne could think of no national costume that included quite that kind of a tunic belted over loose trousers, nor that particular type of sandal. A little shiver slid over him and he stopped just beyond the edge of the lantern-light. The men had not seen him yet, and he was suddenly not sure that he wanted them to. The strangeness began to come through to him, no longer in the mass, but in small casual detail that made it real, and now he began to be afraid, not with his body but with his mind.

From out of the rain and the shadows close by him, someone said, "You must be Trehearne."

The sheer reflex of tight-strung nerves closed Trehearne's grip on the automatic and brought him whirling around. The speaker must have seen the gesture, for he said quietly, "You won't need that. Come back a way, I want to talk to you."

"Who—?"

"Keep your voice down! Come on."

Trehearne followed the blurred figure of a man in a yellow tunic and dark trousers. Even in the gloom he could see that the belt around the man's waist was studded with gems, and the fastenings of his sandals glinted like fireflies in the wet grass. The small shiver twitched again at Trehearne's nerves, and he kept his hand in his pocket, over the comforting prosaic weight of the gun. He had thought at first that the man was Kerrel, but he was too short, and the voice was different. Neither spoke again until they had reached a blank corner of the keep well out of sight of the sheds. Then the man stopped and turned, and Trehearne said, "How did you know me?"

Faint light from an embrasure high above fell on the stranger's face. It was a Vardda face, but it was not beautiful. It was ugly, and kind, with very shrewd eyes and a merry mouth that was not really merry at all, even when it smiled. It was smiling now.

"Your fame has come ahead of you." He nodded toward the wall and what was beyond it. "Kerrel says you won't come, Shairn says you will. They're all betting on you in there." He examined Trehearne closely in the dim light, and shook his head. "I wouldn't have believed it if I hadn't seen it. You really are remarkable."

"I've been told that before," said Trehearne sourly, and glanced at the stone wall, remembering what Shairn had said to him at the cove. An angry glint came into his eyes. "She's sure of herself."

"Shairn is sure of everything, and herself most of all." The man had been drinking, but he was not even slightly

16

drunk. His tone was serious. "Now listen to me, my friend. I've stood around a long while in the rain watching for you when I should have been attending to my business, and I'm breaking a very important law right now. No one else has seen you. Take your horse and ride like hell away from here, and I'll forget that I have." He laid an urgent hand on Trehearne's shoulder. "This may be hard for you to believe, but I'm offering you your life."

The voices of the men rang down the wind, and Trehearne thought of the crates and cases they were bringing up from below as though preparing them for loading, and suddenly an answer came to him.

"Smuggling," he said. "You could land planes out here, and nobody would ever know it."

"Smuggling is precisely it. Now will you go? I haven't any right to do this, but I hate to see a man die just for a woman's amusement."

"Why are you so sure I'll die?"

"Because you're not true Vardda, and more than that I can't tell you. Just please for God's sake go!"

Trehearne thought, He's sincere, he means it, and smuggling isn't all the answer, these aren't common criminals. Something strange, very strange, and maybe he's right . . . The fear that he had had before rose up in him and it was of the body now as well as the mind, a chill premonition of the unnatural. He hesitated, and the ugly man said softly, "Good! I'll get your horse."

There was a creak and a bang and a burst of sound as the great oaken door of the keep swung open. The stranger pressed Trehearne flat against the wall. The doorway was just out of sight, but Trehearne could hear the voices clearly. They were speaking their own unfamiliar tongue, so that what they said was lost to him, but he knew they were talking about him. He heard his name, and the voice that spoke it was Shairn's. Then she laughed. She didn't need to laugh. The sound of her voice would have been enough. Trehearne flung off the stranger's restraining arm and stood away from the wall.

"You fool!" whispered the stranger furiously, and caught at him, but Trehearne was remembering things, words, looks, and the anger in him burned away the fear. He walked out into the light that spilled across the

17

courtyard from the open door. Kerrel and a number of others, mostly women, were standing there, but the only one he saw was Shairn, girdled with jewels and wearing a tunic the color of flame, holding in her hand a goblet of wine. A silence fell, and Shairn's gaze was fixed on his. Even so, he could not read it.

She smiled and said, "Thank you, Michael. I've won my bet."

IV

A HAND FELL UPON TREHEARNE'S SHOULDER FROM BE-hind. It was the man in the yellow tunic, and he had become, in the last few seconds, quite jovially drunk. He gave Trehearne a friendly shove toward the door and called out to the people who stood there, "I found him out here looking for a way in—and I swear the man's a Varddia!" Under his breath he said rapidly in Trehearne's ear, "Keep your mouth shut, or we'll both be in trouble!"

They went together into the keep. The men stared closely at Trehearne, and the woman chattered about him in their own tongue. And Kerrel said to Shairn, "Are you satisfied, now you've got him here?"

"*I* didn't get him here," she said. "He was going to Keregnac anyway, and nothing could have kept him back then." She turned away, toward a table where there were bottles and various foods, and poured wine into a goblet. "Besides, he's a grown man. He knows what he wants to do. Isn't that so, Michael?"

She handed him the goblet. He took it and said, "Oh yes, that's so. You'd better collect your bet."

"I think," she answered, "I'll let it ride." She raised

18

her goblet to sip the wine, doing it in such a way that her sleeve fell back and showed him the dark bruised ring his fingers had left around her wrist.

The man in the yellow tunic said something in his own language, and her eyes narrowed. But she turned to Kerrel and said mildly, "Edri doesn't approve of me."

"I don't think any of us do right now," said Kerrel. "You should have let the man alone."

"Michael doesn't think so—do you, Michael? I didn't tempt him to follow me. That was his idea."

"Well, he followed you," said Edri, and there was a deep anger in his voice.

"But not all the way," murmured Shairn, and smiled into Trehearne's eyes. "Only the first step, Michael. You were annoyed with me when I wouldn't tell you about the Vardda, very much annoyed. So now you're going to find out." She reached up her fingers and drew them slowly across his cheek. "You look like a Vardda, you bear yourself like one, you even think like one. But *are* you one?"

Kerrel said irritably, "That's impossible, and you know it." He began to speak to Edri and the other men, in that language that Trehearne had never heard before. They seemed disturbed and ill at ease, men beset by a problem to which there was no good solution. Their attitude, and the particular way in which the women looked at him, took away the fine edge of Trehearne's excitement. "They act," he said to Shairn, "as though they're planning where to bury me."

She shrugged. "Oh, they're discussing all sorts of alternatives, but there's only one possible answer." She sat down on the edge of the table, watching him in the catlike way that she had. "Nervous?"

"Cold. The rain was very wet." That was only half the truth, but he was damned if he was going to admit it to her. "And I'm curious. Where do you people come from? What are you doing here? What's all the mystery about?"

"Don't be impatient, Michael. It can't all be told at once." She had been listening intently to what the men were saying, and now she rose again. "I think it's time I took a hand in this. Men always talk in circles."

She joined the group. Trehearne finished off his wine

19

and poured more from a queer stone bottle. It was good, but he couldn't place it on any list of vintages. There was beginning to be a nightmare quality about this culmination of his long search. Everything was too business-like, too solemn—and too insane. He wished they would stop talking about him. He wished somebody would explain to him what was going on out here. The voices went on and on, and suddenly he realized that Shairn had shifted into a language he could understand.

"You see?" she was saying to Kerrel. "I can quote the law as well as you. And you know I'm right."

Kerrel muttered, "It seems to me a choice of evils." And he added furiously, "You should have let the man alone!"

"He has a right to his chance," Shairn said. "He came a long way to get it."

"Do I detect a note of malice there?" inquired Edri.

"Detect what you like. Anyway, there is no other course—unless one of you feels up to killing him right here, in cold blood."

Trehearne's wine-glass came down with a clatter on the table, and he thrust his hand into his pocket so that the automatic bulged it very plainly. He said, "You wouldn't find that so easy."

Edri gave a wry sort of shudder and made gestures at him to relax. "We're not violent people," he said. "It's only that you've faced us with a damnably involved problem, and one we've never had to meet before. You see, there are certain laws."

"Laws?"

"Yes." Edri poured himself wine and drank it thirstily, as though to get the taste of something out of his mouth. "Persons above a certain culture level, possessing sufficient I.Q. or influence to be dangerous, are to be permanently silenced if they discover too much about us. Too big an investment, you understand, in Vardda lives as well as money, to be risked—and there are historical reasons for this precaution. But we're extremely careful, and the situation simply hasn't come up before, at least in my time." He sat down, sighing. "And of course, with you there's the added question. Are you or are you not a Vardda? I thought we might appoint you an honorary one, so to speak, and let you work for us

20

here, but that was too big a transgression for Kerrel to swallow." Edri glanced at the tall man—entirely without love, Trehearne thought. "He's an agent of the Council, which means the long arm of the law. So I guess it's settled, Trehearne."

Trehearne's mouth was dry, and the words didn't want to come out of it, but there was a dangerous light in his eyes. "*What* is settled?"

Shairn came before him, her face uplifted, smiling, sweet. "You're coming with us, Michael. That's what you wanted. Aren't you happy?"

"Coming with you—*where?*"

"To Llyrdis."

He did not like her smile. He did not like the wisdom in it, the mockery, the knowledge of things beyond his ken. She bore him malice, and somehow she had got her revenge, and he didn't understand how. All the little details joined together in his mind, the language, the dress, the physical appearance, the taste of a purple wine that came from no familiar vineyard, and they pressed down on him like an avalanche, crowned with the echo of an unknown name, and he was cold deep inside himself, cold with a dread that even yet had no clear shape to it.

He repeated, "Llyrdis?"

"Oh, Christ, don't torture the man," said Edri wearily to Shairn. Then he looked at Trehearne and said, "Llyrdis is our home world, the fourth planet of the star you call Aldebaran."

That was all he said. No one else spoke, there was not a sound inside the ancient room of stone, and even outside all noise had ceased, and the word *Aldebaran* tolled in that silence like a far-off bell. A curious weakness came over Trehearne. Shairn's face grew misty and indistinct. The solid ground, the Earth on which he stood, slipped out from under him and vast yawning windows opened on all sides, windows into space, into darkness and wild light . . .

He said to Edri, quite reasonably, "But that isn't possible."

Somebody put a wine-cup in a hand that didn't belong to him any more, and Edri's voice spoke to him from miles away. "But it is. Drink up, Trehearne. Sovereign remedy for practically everything. Take in the idea slowly, with the wine. We come from another world, another sun. It seems incredible to you. To us, it's only a familiar fact."

Trehearne sat down. The wine burned in his throat, and his head spun round. Everything had turned unreal. "Another world, another sun." He stared down at himself, turning his hands over and back again and staring at them as though he had never seen them before. "My own blood. That's why . . ." He shook his head, stumbling over his own words, and then he shivered, a muscular reaction that shook him right down to his heels. He repeated carefully, "I am going with you."

"Very soon now," said Edri, in such a sombre tone that Trehearne was startled partly out of his daze, enough to see that Edri looked at him with pity, as one looks at a man about to die. A new alarm took hold of Trehearne, and he cried out,

"What's the matter? What are you hiding from me?"

"An ordeal." Once more Shairn stood before him, and her eyes were searching into him, and she had ceased to smile. "You've been given what you wanted, a chance to learn the truth about yourself."

He rose and put his hands on her as he had once before, and not in tenderness. "Go on."

Her red mouth parted a little to show him the edges of her teeth. "Only a true Vardda can endure the velocities of star-flight. Are you afraid, Michael?"

"Yes," he said. "I am." He stood for a long moment, with the blood pounding in his temples and everything, herself, the world, all the years of his own life that had gone before, lost and vague beyond a blinding mist, and then he said slowly, "But you're right, I've got what I wanted."

Outside the keep a man's voice shouted. Someone said, "The ship!" More voices shouted, and the door was flung open. Something dark and cruel came into Trehearne's face. He looked at Shairn and said, "I'll live to thank you." He let her go. People were moving toward the door. He moved with them, as in a dream, but knowing that he would not wake. He lost track of individuals. There were only shadows around him, sounds, motion, without meaning. The walls were gone, and the light. Wet, cold, dark, the outside, the moor, the wind and the naked sky. It had stopped raining. There was a wide rift in the clouds, a valley of stars, and in the valley was a presence, solemn, silent, huge and strange. He watched it, and it settled down, gently as a drift of the night itself, and it sang as it came, a quiet humming that filled all the space between the horizons with a quivering echo more felt than heard. Power. Immensity, and strength. Trehearne drew in a deep unsteady breath. His heartbeats rocked him as he stood. Instinctively his hands moved, a flier's hands, remembering the might of pistons and of jets, groping toward a greater thing. He was not conscious of the motion. He was cold, and the wind flowed through his bones. The great dim bulk dropped down and lay quiet on the moor. Its hull was scored and pitted by the atmospheres of unnamed worlds. Its ports had looked upon infinities where the stars were swallowed up like clouds of fireflies. Trehearne began to walk toward it. If there were others with him, he did not know it. His eyes were on the ship.

A lock-door opened high in the looming flank. White light blazed from it. A folding metal stair came down, and then people descended it and mingled with those that were on the ground. A larger hatch clanged open, lower down. More light blazed out. Machinery began to caltter, and men went back and forth and shouted. The things that were made ready in the sheds began their transfer to the ship. Trehearne reached the foot of the ladder.

He looked up. The vast alien bulk of the ship was above him. It hung over him like the end of the world. It had come out from the darkness between the stars, and it would return there, and he was going with it. There were voices all around him, and some of them were speaking to him, but he did not hear them. He saw no faces. He saw nothing but the curved immensity of the hull that had made such voyages. There were tears in his eyes. They were not of fear, nor of self-pity. They were of exultation. Men had done this thing. Men had reached out and taken the stars in their hands. They were not men of Earth, but they were of his own race. And they had done it.

He began to climb the ladder, and the treads rang hollow beneath his feet.

High. High up in the cold wind, with the smell of the

23

wet moor heavy on it. A round lock-chamber opened before him. He stepped into it, on a metal deck worn bright by the passing of many feet. Others came behind him and pressed him on, down a long transverse corridor faced in metal. The scars of time and hard use were on it. Now and again through a bulkhead door he glimpsed a cabin or an orderly room. They were real. Men lived and worked in them. Someone—Edri—made him turn aside and into a lounge with deep chairs bolted to the deck. "Sit down," said Edri, and he sat obediently. And Edri said, "You have a chance, but you'll have to fight for it. The first time is hard even for . . ." He stopped, and Trehearne finished for him.

"Even for a true Vardda."

"Even," said Edri gently, "for a Vardda. Trehearne, we're alone in the galaxy. Generations ago our race was founded by a man named Orthis, whose system of controlled mutation made us what we are, the Vardda—the Starmen. It's a difference, a condition of the flesh. With us there is no doubt. With you—your blood is mixed. But you're a throwback in every other way. The mutation may have bred true, also."

His voice carried hope, but no conviction. Trehearne frowned, trying to grasp the sense of what he said. It was hard to think, hard to believe with his mind, in spite of what his senses told him. Things had happened too fast. Too fast, and too big. He caught a glimpse of Shairn's face. It was white, and he realized that all at once she was beginning to be afraid.

"Fight," said Edri. "That's the thing to remember."

All through the ship, bells rang sharply.

Trehearne took hold of the arms of the chair in which he sat. For a brief moment of panic he wanted to get up and run, but he could hear the sonorous clang of the lock-doors closing and he knew it was no use. Everyone was seated now. The bells rang again. He braced himself, and fixed his gaze on Shairn.

Swift, smooth and awesome as the hand of God, acceleration pressed down upon him. Muttering an all but silent thunder, the ship rushed upward into the sky, and for the first time in histroy, Earth-born ears listened to the banshee scream of atmosphere past a cleaving hull.

24

V

THE WAILING SHRIEK ROSE TO A CRESCENDO, AND THEN it died. Earth was gone. They had stepped away from it. Even its sky was behind them. A weight like the weight of mountains lay on Trehearne, and he was horribly afraid.

He waited for the pressure to ease. His temples were bursting, it was an agony to breathe, and he thought, It can't go on like this, it's got to let up! But it did not. There was a change in the pitch of the motor vibration. He listened to it climb, higher and higher, until it slipped over the threshold of hearing, and as it climbed, the pressure grew. The bones of his chest crushed in upon his lungs. Everything around him began to waver and grow vague, to recede slowly into a reddish twilight.

And still the pressure grew.

Something was happening to him. Something unearthly and strange. He was a flier, a test-pilot. He had known pressure before. He had taken all the gravs a power-diving plane could bear and he had never come near blacking out. But this was different. He felt it in the fibres, the very atoms of his being. This was velocity beside which the velocities of the fastest jets were as nothing. This was the speed of interstellar flight. And he could feel it tearing at the separate cells of his flesh, riving them apart, rending the tissues of physical existence. *A difference, a condition of the flesh. With us there is no doubt, but you . . .*

Anguish became terror, terror turned into blind panic. His body was shredding apart, dissolving toward a tattered ruin, a heap of bloody rags. This body he had been so proud of, this star-born self that was only a

25

mockery, a sham. The mutation hadn't been bred true. He was going to die, to cease utterly from being. He was . . .

Far, far away, a voice, Shairn's voice, crying, "I've killed him. Poor Michael, I didn't mean for him to die!"

Poor Michael. A mongrel, a walking deceit. Proud Michael, who thought he was so damned good, and wasn't anything. Idiot Michael, who had run after a witch. And she hadn't meant for him to die. She hadn't really been that angry because he had treated her like an equal—not nicely perhaps, but like an equal, which he wasn't. That was kind of her, not really to want him killed. He began to be able to see her face again. He wasn't sure whether it was true sight, or only the memory of how she had looked before he began to die. But he could see her, pale, distorted. He was glad he could see her. She was sitting in front of him, and she wasn't far away. Somehow, pressure or no pressure, he was going to get to her. He was going to put his hands around her white throat, and then they could forget about star-flight together, and it wouldn't matter that he was a mongrel and she was not. He began to fight against the pressure.

He wanted so little. Only to get up, to move the short distance and lock his fingers at the back of her neck, with his two thumbs lying over the great pulses. So little. He was filled with a raging determination to have it. He fought. He had nothing to fight with but will-power and the instinctive desire of the organism to claw onto life as long as there was a flicker of it left. He wanted to get up, and he fought, an inner struggle without sound or motion, a blind battle to regain control of his own flesh. His face contorted, like the face of a man who lifts something far too heavy, and the sweat ran on it. Slowly, slowly, his hands moved on the chair arms, contracted, became fists. The muscles of his arms tightened, and then the great muscles of the chest and belly, and they labored, and the breath came painfully into his lungs— came, and went, and came again, and his flagging heart stumbled, steadied, and began to beat more evenly. The red mist that wrapped him cleared away a bit and he could see Shairn more distinctly. She was staring at him. Her mouth and eyes were wide open, ludicrous, startled. Then Edri's head came between them and blot-

26

ted her out, and he was shouting, but the blood was pounding so loud in Trehearne's ears that he could not hear what he said. He raised a hand and tried to thrust Edri away. He did not want to lose sight of Shairn. There was a tremendous exaltation on him. He was winning. He was going to get up and do the thing he wanted to do. The sinews coiled and tensed along his thighs. The pressure didn't hurt so much, and the terrible vibrations of speed were not tearing at him quite so hard. He leaned forward a little, breathing in deep harsh gasps, and his body strained and tightened . . .

"He's going to live, he's made it. Michael . . ."

Shairn's voice, thin and shrill through the tumult in his ears. For a moment the meaning didn't penetrate. Then slowly it dawned on him what she had said. And then, more slowly still, he realized that it was true. He could feel the life flowing back into him. He was getting the hang of it now, a simple matter of tensing the muscles in a certain way, and the agony of vibration lessened, the atoms of his body stopped their ghastly dissolution. It was only a matter of strength—not the kind that can move great weights, but a more subtle kind, a tensile strength that knit the fabric of the flesh together and made it impervious as steel. In an infantile way he had been using it for years without knowing it, in his testing of fast planes. That was why he had never blacked out, why he had never been tortured as other men were by the spectre of inertia waiting for them at the end of a dive. Now he had found at last the purpose his body was made for. He forgot about Shairn. She didn't matter any more. He had won, he was alive, he was going to live, and he was not a sham nor mockery, he was not even a mongrel. The mutation had bred true. His vision was clearing fast. He raised his head and looked around, and they were all staring at him, the Vardda, the Starmen, who had been so sure he was going to die. They were talking back and forth in excited voices, they were getting up and coming toward him, and Edri was pounding him on the shoulder. He thrust them all away and stood up.

"I'm one of you now," he said. "I passed your test." He was suddenly exhausted and shaken, but he would not show it. He stood erect and faced them.

Shairn took him in her arms and kissed him. Trehearne said, "You're glad I didn't die."

"Yes. Oh, yes!"

"You would have felt just a little guilty, wouldn't you?" He held her off and looked at her. She was very beautiful. Her throat was warm and white. He studied it, thinking what he had wanted to do only a few short minutes ago, and then he shook his head. He said slowly, "I owe you something, Shairn. I won't forget it."

She did not like his tone, and her brows drew into a dark line. She turned away, and over her shoulder Trehearne saw Kerrel looking at him in such an intent, strange way that he challenged it. "You don't look very happy, Kerrel. Does my survival upset you?"

Kerrel shook his head. "I don't enjoy condemning a man, particularly when I have nothing against him. But it brings up other problems. You have no conception of them now, Trehearne, but the thing you have just done brings you automatically into conflict with the most basic tenet of Vardda law, and how the Council will decide the question, I don't know." He shifted his gaze to Edri and said in a curiously soft tone, "It could have the most dangerous consequences."

If it was bait, Edri refused to take it. He laughed and said, "This is no time to worry about consequences. I'm going to find Trehearne a cabin and me a bottle, and put the two together for a small celebration. A man doesn't become a Vardda every day." He took Trehearne's elbow and started him toward the door. "Come on."

Trehearne's new-found strength had not deserted him —it was, apparently, automatic when it was once started, like the heart-beat—but the ordinary kind was running out of him like water from a sieve. He made it out into the passageway without staggering, but a few steps farther on he clung to the bolt-heads in the wall and said unhappily, "I think I'm going to fall over."

"Reaction," said Edri. "Don't let it bother you. We all get it, first time out. Here, hang on."

The passage seemed a mile long, but eventually there was a cabin, small, compact, and functional, and there was a bunk, and Trehearne sat down on it. Edri went away somewhere, and came back again after a minute with a bottle. The stuff, whatever it was, went down like

28

white fire, and Trehearne felt better. He set the cup aside and then began to look at his hands, turning them over as though he had never seen them before.

"They seem like everybody else's," he said.

"They're not. You're not. As Kerrel told you, you have no idea yet of what you've done, but as time goes by you will."

"It's quite true, then—about the mutation?"

"Oh, yes, quite. The form and structure of your body cells, and mine, are different from other people's. Due to that altered form and structure, your tissues, and mine, possess a tensile strength in their cell-walls that can withstand incredible acceleration pressure without collapse. And I hope you never know how lucky you were that the mutation was a recessive gene that finally bred true in you." He filled the glasses again, slowly, withdrawn for a moment into some brooding thought of his own. Then he added somberly, "Some day I'll tell you the story of Orthis, who found the secret of the mutation. And a grand proud story it is, but with a shameful ending. He . . . No. Forget it. The less you know about that, the better. Besides, we're celebrating. Drink up."

Trehearne drank. His head was swimming, and he felt hollow inside. The glass was heavy in his hands. He said, "There'll be trouble when I get to—to Llyrdis?"

"Sufficient unto the day, Trehearne. Worry about that when you come to it."

But he had already ceased to worry. Llyrdis. He said the name again, and it felt strange on his tongue. Llyrdis. A name and a world he had never heard of until a few short hours ago, and now . . . The hollow spaces inside him were filled suddenly with homesickness, with a longing, with something akin to horror. He stared at the iron walls that closed him in, and he knew where he was, in an impossible ship with alien people, flying faster than light across nothingness to an alien star . . . His stomach contracted, sending up a bitter fluid to burn his throat, and his hands were cold as a dead man's. Earth was gone. His Earth, sky, mountains, sunrise, city streets, country roads, the faces and voices of people, the men he had worked with, the women he had had or wanted to have, all the familiar things—the currency, the bars, the names of nations, books, pictures, shirtmakers,

29

history—what was the use now of all the history he had learned, where did Caesar rank among the stars? Earth was gone, and even the sun had gone with it, and it was in a way as though he had died—and how do you start life again afterward, a stranger? There was this cabin, and outside its walls there was no world, no sunlight, nothing. Nothing.

Nothing . . .

Edri led him swiftly to a tiny adjoining cubicle and left him alone with his misery while he used the inter-com by the cabin door. Presently the ship's doctor joined him. They got Trehearne back into the bunk, and a needle glittered briefly in the light, sending him to a place where there were not even any dreams.

On Number Four screen in the ship's control room, the pinpoint fleck that represented an isolated yellow sun flickered, faded, and went out.

VI

TREHEARNE LOOKED UP FROM THE BUNK AND ASKED, "How long have I slept?"

"Nearly twenty-four hours by Earth reckoning," Edri answered. "You needed it." He leaned over and offered Trehearne a prosaic pack of American cigarettes. "Smoke?"

Trehearne took one and sat up. He smoked for some time in silence, remembering. Finally he said, "It all happened, didn't it?"

Edri nodded.

"I know it must have, but I don't believe it." Trehearne shook his head. "Of all the incredible . . . What were you doing there, Edri? How can you come and go on Earth without anyone knowing? What are the Vard-da, besides—well, mutants?"

"Traders. Merchants. The most commercial race in the galaxy." Edri lifted the cover off a tray on a small table by the bunk. "I brought your breakfast. Go ahead and eat while I gabble. How we come and go is fairly simple. We land at odd intervals, here and there in the waste spaces of which Earth has a number. We do our business, and after a while are picked up again. As I told you before, we're exceedingly careful, and the fact that hardly anyone on Earth would believe the truth if they were told it is a protection. Of course, trading in secret that way, we're limited in what we can take, and Earth exports—the genuine articles and not mere copies —command very high prices. You'd be amazed at the value of French perfumes, Scotch whiskey, and American films on planets you never heard of."

"Do you trade with them all in secret?"

"Good Lord, no! Most worlds, even the very primitive ones, we can deal with quite openly. They might not like us, but they benefit enormously from our commerce."

"Then why not Earth?"

"Well," said Edri, "I don't like to offend your sensibilities as a native of the place, but Earth is a crazy planet. Oh, it's not the only one. There's a number of them scattered about, and we avoid open contact with all of them. You see, Trehearne, most worlds develop, or remain undeveloped, more or less homogeneously in the matter of civilization. I don't mean they're entirely peaceful, because they're not, but in the long run their populations are more predictable, more stable than on the Earth-type worlds that have grown up all out of joint. You know what I mean—on one side of the world atomic power, on the other the wooden plough and the blowgun. Too big a gap, and it makes trouble all down the line. Now, a primitive society regards war as a sport and takes an honest pleasure in it. A society in a high state of culture regards it as something outgrown and obsolete as hunting game for food. Everybody knows where they are. But when you get a world with great big overlapping mobs of population, every one of them in a different stage of cultural development and every one of them subject to a constant bombardment of outside stimuli they can't assimilate, you have got a mixture that keeps exploding in all directions. We have a healthy desire not to get blown up, and besides, it's impossible to establish any profitable trade with a world continually torn by wars. So—does that answer your question?"

"I take it," Trehearne said sourly, "that the Vardda don't think much of Earth."

"It's a good world. It'll settle down some day. Nobody can fight forever. They either knock themselves back into barbarism again, or they grow up."

Trehearne put down the fork on the empty plate, and looked at Edri, rather angrily. "Don't the Vardda ever fight?" he demanded. "I gather there's a vast commercial empire. There must be trade wars, battles over markets and rights. No empire was ever built without them."

"No other empire was ever built," said Edri quietly, "without any competition. I think you still don't quite understand. We have an absolute, complete, and unbreakable monopoly on interstellar flight. Only the Vardda ships go between the stars, and only the Vardda men can fly them. You know the reason, you proved it in yourself. We don't have to fight."

Trehearne let go a long, low whistle. "And we thought we had monopolies on Earth! But I don't see why, if you could mutate, others couldn't do it, too. How do you hold them down?"

"We don't hold anybody down. We don't rule, influence, or interfere with any world but our own. We learned long ago that it was bad business. As to the mutation, it's impossible. The secret of the process was lost with Orthis, some thousand years ago." He rose abruptly from the chair where he had been sitting, and pointed to some garments in the locker. "I think those will fit you. Get dressed, and I'll show you around."

Trehearne looked doubtfully at the clothes, a tunic of dark green silk, dark trousers, a modestly jewelled belt, and sandals. Edri grinned.

"You'll get used to them. And you won't feel half as peculiar as you would look going about in those ridiculous tweeds."

Trehearne shrugged, and put them on. He had to admit they were comfortable. There was a mirror set inside the locker door, and he studied himself in it. He was startled to see how changed he was in the Vardda dress. The last vestige of Earth was gone.

Still looking into the mirror, he said, "Edri . . ."

"Yes?"

"I am a Vardda now. I've proved it. What can they do to me, on Llyrdis?"

"I wish I could tell you. Actually, you are a true Vardda, a complete atavism. But legally—that's another thing. That basic tenet of Vardda law that Kerrel referred to is a prohibition against admitting into our race non-Vardda strains of any kind. Keeping the Vardda blood pure isn't just pride, it's an economic necessity, and the one unbreakable tabu. The solution of that puzzle will be up to the Council, and my advice is to forget it until then. Come on, and I'll give you something else to think about."

Trehearne was glad enough to go. The lost, sick, nightmarish feeling was creeping back on him again, and he was glad of any diversion. They went out into the corridor, and he followed Edri forward. He became aware of a deep inner vibration of power that filled the ship, a sort of humming drone that seemed to challenge the whole universe to make it stop. It sang in his ears, in his blood and his quivering nerve-ends, and the excitement he had felt when he first saw the ship returned to him full force. This was the ultimate. All his life he had been playing with children's toys, but here, under his feet and all around him, was the highest dream of men.

"What's the motive power? What's the principle? And how can you go faster than light? The limiting speed, contraction, mass . . ."

Edri laughed. "One at a time, please. And such simple little questions, too! It took centuries to evolve a technology capable of answering them, and you want me to explain it all in a few words. Well, a few words is all I know about it. I'm a drinker by profession, not a scientist. Anyway, a really functional ship, whether it plies water, air, or space, must get its motive power by reacting against the element it travels in. And so, right now, the big atomic-powered generators in the stern are producing fifth-order rays which react against the fabric of space itself. And space, not wishing to be torn apart,

33

obligingly thrusts us onward. Very simple, I believe, once you know the trick."

Trehearne grunted.

"As to limiting speeds," said Edri, "the Vardda scientists used to believe in them too—until they got to playing around with cosmotrons. One day a particle they were experimenting with upset them horribly by going much faster than light, and that's how they discovered the fifth-order rays. They found out, as your scientists will find, that the theoretical absolutes you set up from limited knowledge will prove illusory when your knowledge expands. I could explain all that to you if I knew continuum-mechanics better than I do!"

"I couldn't understand it anyway," said Trehearne, "so it's just as well."

They had reached the forward end of the corridor. There was a narrow circular stairway leading up. Edri stood back and motioned Trehearne to climb it. He did, fighting down another attack of the shakes on the way —you couldn't take it all in, you couldn't get used to it all at once, the strangeness, the utter separation from everything that had been, the headlong plunge into alien horizons, for a long time you were going to get panicky when you thought about it. He emerged into a round observation dome of immensely heavy quartz. He didn't know what he had expected to see, but he was disappointed. There was nothing to be seen at all but darkness, streaked with creeping lines of light.

"Those are stars," said Edri, who had come up behind him. "Or rather, the radiation patterns of stars. At our present velocity we're overtaking the lines of luminous energy they have left behind them. Star-tracks, we call them."

He closed a switch, and the thick quartzite became suffused with a pallid, milky glow. Edri consulted a master dial, and made adjustments.

"Watch the dome," he said. "It's triple thickness, of a special molecular composition, each plane laid at a different oblique angle. I've switched high-frequency electronic current into hair-line grids between the three planes and all sorts of interesting and complicated things are happening in the molecular structure of the quartzite."

Trehearne watched. His heart was beating hard.

"Behold," said Edri, "the light-impulses of the star-tracks are caught, stepped up, wrenched about, and finally held on the inner lens."

Trehearne beheld, and beholding, he forgot Edri and the ship and himself. He forgot Earth, the past, and the future. He forgot almost to breathe.

Edri's voice came to him softly. "You may see this often, Trehearne, but never again for the first time."

Trehearne barely heard him. The ship had fallen away beneath him, leaving him suspended in the plunging gulfs that lie between the island stars, and he looked awestruck into the dark and splendid loneliness of space.

Through the magic of that quartzite dome he saw the great suns march in flame and thunder on their way around the ouroboros curve of infinity. Some were solitary hunters, others were joined together in companies of stars. He saw their cosmic pageant of life and death, the young suns blazing with a blue-white strength, the golden suns, the old red suns, the dead suns black with funeral ash. He saw the far-off galaxies, the coiling fires of the nebulae, the wonderful terrifying nations of the Milky Way streaming along the rim of creation. And as he looked the last of thought and feeling went from him and he was like a child still dazed from birthing.

Some of the stars, perhaps, he recognized—Algol beating like a bloody heart, the splintered glory of Sirius. Orion strode gigantic across the gulfs, girded with suns, and dead ahead, tipping the far-flung Hyades, Aldebaran burned in sullen splendor.

Aldebaran. Another sun. Other worlds, other peoples, other ways of life. He was going there, a stranger.

A deep tremor shook him. Time went by, but he took no notice of it. He was a man lost, sunk and drowned in infinity. Edri watched him, with a certain sadness. After a while he pulled the switch again, and the dome went blank, showing only the flat darkness and the crawling streaks of light. Trehearne sighed, but he did not move. Edri smiled, and shook him. Trehearne turned slowly, and when Edri led the way back down the stair he followed, but without knowing where he was going or why.

The passageway was empty. Edri stopped and waited

until Trehearne's eyes focussed on him with some semblance of understanding.

"I'm going," he said, "to break a life-long habit and say something important. Are you listening?"

Trehearne nodded.

"You'll be spending a lot of time with the others, which will inevitably mean with Shairn. Keep away from her, Trehearne. No matter whether you love her or hate her, stay away."

Trehearne smiled. His head was ringing with stars, his vision was dazzled by the blaze of nebulae.

"Shairn doesn't look to me like much of a permanent deal for anybody."

"That's the trouble. Kerrel talked her into this flying jaunt around with him to break up the games she was playing with somebody else on Llyrdis. He's put up with an awful lot from her, and he's not the type at all— which makes people wonder."

"What?"

"Well, Kerrel's an agent of the Council, highly respected, got a lot of influence and so on, but we Vardda count our wealth in ships, and Kerrel's poor. Shairn inherited thirty, the fourth largest fleet in space. In other words, he's got more than Shairn to lose."

"He can keep her," Trehearne said. "And her ships."

"You don't know the lady. I do. And I can tell you that staying away from her is no easy job when she doesn't want to be stayed away from."

"Oh, the heck with her," said Trehearne impatiently. It was a long way down from the stars to petty gossip, and it annoyed him. "I don't see what it's got to do with me anyway."

"I told you, I know the lady. And I know Kerrel. He's your enemy already—"

Trehearne was amazed. "Why?"

"Because it's his duty to be. Because the whole structure of the Vardda society, which he is sworn to protect, is based on a few ironclad rules, and you're liable to break every one of them. Oh, it isn't just you. There are larger isues involved—I'll explain them, but that'll take time—and you're sort of automatically mixed up with them. Kerrel is a just man as he sees it, but his justice is not tempered with mercy. I've seen him in action too often, Trehearne. You'll have trouble enough. Don't give him a personal motive, too."

Edri's manner was so serious that Trehearne began to feel uneasy. A great blank wall rose up before him, behind which lay the life and complexities, the politics and philosophies and contentions of the Vardda state, and he couldn't see through it or over it. He said, "I've got an awful lot to learn. It scares me, how much. You and Kerrel don't exactly love each other, do you?"

Edri shrugged. "He suspects me of harboring ideas not in agreement with his own. On Llyrdis as it is on Earth, Trehearne, beware of a man with a belief." Suddenly he laughed. "Well, that's enough of that. As you just remarked, you have a lot to learn. We might as well get started."

Trehearne followed him obediently, to begin his reeducation as a Vardda.

VII

IT WAS AMAZING HOW QUICKLY EARTH, WITH ALL ITS habits and memories, slipped away from Trehearne. The pangs and wrenchings of homesickness still came to him now and then, mostly when he lay alone in his bunk, just before sleep. But they were less and less violent. He began to have for his native world the nostalgic affection one has for a foster-parent far less than perfect, but all the same a part of one's life—a part done with now, but with its bright and kindly interludes to look back upon. He was not sorry that he had left it. By a freak of genetics he had been born an alien, and he had never fitted there. Now, rapidly and easily, he was finding himself.

At first there were periods when he felt that he was dreaming, that the ship and all within it would disappear and he would waken. But as his mind readjusted itself, shaking free from the narrow horizons where it had been prisoned, ancestral pride and ancestral longing began to stir. And with that stirring came an insatiable hunger for knowledge.

Edri was his chief teacher. For some reason, the ugly man with the unhappy eyes and unfailing cheerfulness of speech had taken a liking to him, and Trehearne was glad of it. He needed friends. But there were others, too. Men and women, mostly young, healthy and full of themselves, loving the life they lived and enjoying to the hilt his own wide-eyed reactions to it. For a while they regarded him very much as he would have regarded an animal that had suddenly learned to talk and do sums, but they got used to him, and there was never any malice in their conduct. He liked them. They were his kind of people. They *were* his people.

Kerrel remained civil, but aloof. Shairn spoke to him when she felt like it, as casually as though they had known each other all their lives and nothing of interest had ever happened between them. But sometimes he thought she looked at him in a way that was not casual at all, and he could not tell what she was thinking. He played along. It was hard, when he got to remembering things. But he did it. And he had enough to do to keep his mind off women. There weren't hours enough in the ship's day to supply him.

He learned the Vardda tongue. He learned the rudiments of Vardda history and the outlines of their social structure. But most of all, with an inborn sureness, he learned the Vardda mind, the Vardda point of view, and his own character expanded, having found a meaning for itself. He was a Vardda, and they were the Starmen —Galactic Man, as Edri had put it once, a unique species, specialized and fitted for the most splendid work of all, the conquest of the stars.

The power, the magnificence of that voyaging! No wonder the little ships and little skies of Earth had seemed so futile. This was his heritage, the freedom of the stars, the long, long roads of outer space, the swift

38

ships plying between the island continents of suns, the windless, timeless, boundless gulf that washed the shores of a galaxy.

He haunted the ship's bridge, studying the intricate controls and cracking his brain over the staggering complexities of astrogation. In the generator rooms he learned by heart the pulse of the ship, listening to the silence of free flight after acceleration was complete. He deviled the engineers, the pilots, the technicians, with questions, understanding less than half of what they told him but always avid for more. He learned much, and yet it was nothing, and he was mad for learning, mad to hold under his own hands one of these proud giants of the starways.

The Vardda understood him. His hunger was their own, but they had not been barred from satisfaction. They accepted him. They loved to talk, and Trehearne had no lack of language teachers. His head spun to the tales they told him, of travels around the galaxy, of foreign words and happenings in far-off clusters of suns, of dead stars wheeling forever dark through darkness with their frozen worlds, of the sudden dreadful flaring of the novae, of what happens when a ship collides with a rogue star at many times the speed of light.

Trehearne was happy. He was living again as a child lives, in a world of wonders, where everything was new and bright and as yet untarnished. But one dark cloud hung over him—the threat of Vardda law and the Council. They might still take away from him all he had found. That threat got bigger and blacker the closer he came to the end of the voyage, and by the time the ship actually went into deceleration it had grown until it blotted out the whole horizon.

He had learned more now. He understood how the whole vast structure of Vardda economy rested on the unassailable position of the Starmen themselves and their unique ability to endure interstellar velocities. In this case, the blood, the race, was everything. There could not be any compromises, there could not be any challenges of that superiority. And here was he, Earthborn of Earth stock, with only a set of bastard genes to link him with the Vardda, a compromise and a challenge in himself.

39

"But damn it," he said furiously to Edri, "they can't refuse me now! And why, when you come right down to it, would one Vardda more or less make that much difference? The mutation process has been lost anyway, I certainly can't infect anybody else with it, and I don't see what they're afraid of."

Edri gave him a sombre look. "Listen, Trehearne, I haven't helped myself any by being friendly to you, as it is, and I'm not going to make matters worse for both of us by talking treason into the bargain. If you want the full, official answer to that question, go ask Kerrel."

"I will."

He found Kerrel in the lounge, engaged with Shairn and several other people in the complicated game that seemed to serve the Vardda in the place of bridge. Inside a gigantic crystal globe were suspended a number of little solar systems. Activated by magnetic currents, the tiny suns wheeled along and their planets spun in orbits around them, and it was a dizzying thing to look at. Within this microcosm were a dozen or so tiny ships, operated by the players by remote control, and for hazards there were miniature nebulae, dark clouds, and tiny comets. The object was to move the ships about without losing any, one team racing the opposing team's fleet to a selected destination. Trehearne had played a few times, but with no success whatever.

"I want to talk to you," he said, and Kerrel motioned him to wait. Very rapidly and skillfully he pressed a series of buttons on the control board in front of him. Inside the globe a ship depressed its arc, allowing a sparkling comet to pass safely above it, skirted the edge of a dark nebula, shifted course thirty-five degrees and made a perfect landing on a flying worldlet no larger than a pebble. At the top of Kerrel's panel a signal light glowed green.

Beside him Shairn lost two ships in collision and got two red lights for her pains, the "wrecks" being automatically retired out of play. Shairn wasn't watching the globe. She was watching Trehearne, and her eyes were very bright.

Kerrel turned over his place to another man and stood up. "The library's quiet," he said. "We can talk there." He went away with Trehearne. Behind them, Shairn gave up her board and followed.

The ship's library was small, with microbooks racked on the walls. They were mostly technical books, and Trehearne hadn't been able to get much out of them. He had struggled with a few on the theory and practical operation of star-ships, but it was a hopeless job and he hadn't pursued it. His vocabulary was still limited, and even if it hadn't been the technology involved was miles over his head.

Now he faced Kerrel and said, "I asked Edri a question, and he referred me to you. So I'll ask it again. Why would the Vardda Council be afraid to accept me?"

Kerrel put his hands on the back of a chair and thought a minute. "You understand the Vardda position among all the other races of the galaxy."

"Yes. And I don't see how I could possibly alter it."

"Then your understanding isn't complete. There are many worlds in space, Trehearne. Countless millions of people live on them. Do you know how they feel about us?"

"I hadn't thought."

"They hate us. They envy us. It's natural enough. They're prisoned in their own solar systems, forced to watch strangers carry on all their commerce with other stars. But natural or not, it's a factor we have to reckon with."

Trehearne said impatiently, "What can they do about it? They can't mutate, and they can't even try to force you to share the process with them. The thing was lost a thousand years ago. You're safe."

"There are still Orthists."

"Who are they?"

Kerrel looked mildly surprised. "I thought Edri would have told you. No? But you have, of course, heard of Orthis, the discoverer of the mutational process. He was a great man, Trehearne. A brilliant man, a genius, the founder of our race. But he was not a practical man. He lived alone too much in space, worked alone too long in his laboratory-ship. He didn't know human beings, he didn't understand the hard grimy necessities of life, the law of self-preservation. He wanted to give the mutation —and the freedom of the stars—to everyone."

41

He paused, as though he were waiting for Trehearne to speak. But Trehearne, though he was thinking hard, kept his mouth shut.

"Orthis," Kerrel said, "was not able to see what, fortunately, others did see—that giving the mutation to all the races of the galaxy would mean wars and conflicts of such staggering dimensions that whole solar systems, including ours, might very well be destroyed. He clung stubbornly to his views and eventually fled from Llyrdis in defiance of the government, determined to have his own way. He was pursued, of course, and driven away from his objective, so that his attempt failed, but he was never captured. He vanished far out on the rim of the galaxy, and the process went with him. And that's where the trouble is, Trehearne. Some time later Orthis sent back a certain message, which gave his adherents hope that his ship had not been destroyed, that it was, in fact, waiting somewhere to be found again, and the process with it. Now, after a thousand years, they still hope."

Trehearne shook his head. "I certainly can't tell them where the ship is. So how does it affect me?"

"Don't you see how you could be used? An alien, a mongrel, but able to fly the stars—the effect on the Orthist movement would be tremendous, and not only on Llyrdis. People all over the galaxy, wanting what we have, would take you up as a symbol of what they consider their emancipation. I have a lively imagination, but it balks at trying to conceive all the trouble that could breed out of that situation."

A cold sensation was creeping over Trehearne, centering in the pit of his stomach. What Kerrel said made sense. He hated to admit it, but it made sense. He said harshly, "All right, but there must be a way around it. Around me, I mean. I take it that the Vardda Council is made up of politicians, and a politician can get around anything he wants to."

"They can," said Shairn from the doorway. "Particularly when the right people convince them they should."

Both men swung around, surprised. She strolled in, smiling at them impartially. Trehearne made nothing out of it but a smile, but Kerrel's face went suddenly hard.

"I don't know," she said to Trehearne, "whether anyone has mentioned it, but I'm quite an influential person on Llyrdis."

Kerrel said, "Would you mind very much leaving us alone?"

"Yes. You see, Kerrel, I feel rather possessive about him. It's my fault in a way he's here, and I'm going to look out for him, whether he likes it or not."

"That's fine," Trehearne said. "That puts me right in the middle."

"You're there anyway. Isn't he, Kerrel?"

"Shairn, I don't wish to quarrel with you here——"

"I'm not going to quarrel. I'm only stating a fact. Michael has developed into a very proper Vardda, and I don't intend to have him tucked away on Thuvis until he's done something to warrant it."

Kerrel said, as though it were a statement and not a question, "You're going to make an issue of this."

"I'm going to fight you for him. You need to be fought with, Kerrel. You're getting too sure of practically everything."

He moved until he stood in front of her. Trehearne had never seen anyone so angry, and so thoroughly under control. In that moment he began to understand that Kerrel was a dangerous man. Shairn drew a deep breath and threw her head back, and Trehearne knew that she had thought about this for a long time, planning it, working it out, waiting for the chance, and that she was happy about it. It wasn't himself and whether he lived or died. He was only the convenient peg. This was Kerrel and Shairn and a long situation.

Kerrel said, "I've taken a great deal from you, Shairn, but there's a limit. I've reached it."

"I hoped you'd feel that way."

He stood looking at her, and she did not speak, meeting his gaze steadily and with a queer kind of amusement. Finally Kerrel said, "I wish you hadn't done it this way. Not for him. Not for a——"

"But Kerrel," she told him gently, "it had to be something like this, or you wouldn't take no for an answer. I know. I've been trying for the longest time."

Kerrel turned and went out. He said nothing more, and he did not even glance at Trehearne as he passed him. Trehearne looked after him and shivered.

43

"You've been a great help to me," he said bitterly to Shairn. "The first time you didn't quite get me killed, but I believe now you're going to make it."

"Kerrel isn't that important. All he can do is recommend, and he'd have recommended Thuvis anyway." She laughed. "I feel wonderful. He was really beginning to weigh on me."

"Congratulations. And what is Thuvis?"

"I'll show you." She searched along the wall racks until she found the spool she wanted and clipped it into a viewer. "This is the astro-manual for a sector of space that is fortunately very little used. Here, have a look."

Trehearne bent over the magnilens. Equations were gliding slowly across it to the whirring of the unwinding spool, coordinates of a position in space.

"We have no capital punishment on Llyrdis," she said. "Matter of fact, we have very few criminals. But such as there are are sent into permanent exile, here."

She pressed a stud, and the whirring stopped. On the lens was the picture of a dim red sun lost in a dark wilderness, with hardly a distant star to break the desolation. Around it circled one lonely planet, grey, forlorn, and hopeless.

After a long while Trehearne said, "But I'm not a criminal. They couldn't—"

"They could judge you a danger to society, as they judge the Orthists. Kerrel will do his best to put you there—as a matter of principle."

Dying star, and dying world, alone on the edge of nothing. Trehearne looked at it. "What do they do there?"

"Nothing. They just wait."

"For what?"

He knew the answer before she told him. No more ships, no more voyaging, nothing to look forward to but the only release there was. Trehearne drew back from the viewer. Shairn smiled.

"Afraid?"

"Yes."

"I'm on your side."

"Are you? Or are you just using me to punish Kerrel, because he bores you?"

"Don't you trust me?"

"No!"

"But there isn't much you can do about it, is there?"

"I guess not."

"Then you might as well make the best of it."

VIII

THE LONG ARC OF DECELERATION WAS COMPLETED. THE starship was cruising now at planetary speed. Aldebaran had grown from a remote point of fire to a giant sun, terrifyingly near at hand. The small companion was visible only as a faint disc above the upper limb, its bluish light drowned out in the flooding ruddy blaze of the larger star.

The Vardda had crowded up into the observation dome, eager for the first glimpse of home. A heavy shield now covered the dome to sunward and in its shadow the returning travellers pressed and chattered. Trehearne stood among them, listening to their excitement and feeling at a loss in it. Their talk was the talk of strangers, full of names and references that were meaningless to him, strident with a joy he could not share. They were coming home, and he was homeless, the loneliest man in the galaxy. Before him loomed the imagined faces of the Vardda Council, passing judgment, and beyond them in the desolate wastes of space the dying world of Thuvis waited.

Shairn tugged at his sleeve. "There!" she cried. "There it is, Michael. Llyrdis!"

He followed her pointing hand, squinting against the tawny glare, and saw a golden planet wheeling toward them, bright and beautiful, with a trio of circling moons. Suddenly the majesty and splendor of this landing out of space swept over him, and drove away his fears. It was an awesome, a godlike thing, to come into a solar system from outside, drenched in the naked blazing of a foreign sun, and see the planets from far off, no bigger than a child's ball, circling the parent star in their slow eternal orbits. He became as excited as the Vardda, but for a different reason. Presently he would stand on the soil of a strange world, in the light of an alien sun, and the winds that blew would come from far peaks nameless to him, and off of unknown oceans. He watched with the others, as tensely as they.

Edri looked at his face, and smiled. "Mirris is on the other side of the sun, but if you'll look hard off there to your right you'll see Suumis, the outer one of our two immediate neighbors."

Suumis appeared against the farther reaches of space like a little red apple, accompanied by a throng of sparkling motes that Trehearne knew must be moons. He stared at it, trying to realize that the little red apple was a world as big as Earth, gave it up, and turned back again to Llyrdis. It had grown. It fairly leaped toward them as the ship swept in upon it, and Trehearne began to make out misty continents and the shadow-forms of oceans, wrapped in a cloud-shot atmosphere that burned a reddish gold in Aldebaran's light. Then it was closer still, it filled the sky, it spread out monstrously and began to fall . . .

Edri laughed. "Optical illusion. But a striking one, isn't it?"

Trehearne braced his knees and said it was. His heart was in his throat, the rest of his insides had fallen away somewhere, and the ship was plunging at a terrible speed to meet the toppling planet. It touched the atmosphere, and went into it as into a bath of fire. Down it went, rushing, tearing down with a long triumphant scream, and in the lower air the clouds rolled and whipped in golden fury where the dark hull clove them. Trehearne shut his eyes. When he opened them again the ship was sweeping low over an ocean the color of hammered brass, and at length he saw ahead a low shore, and beyond it a rolling plain girdled with tall mountains. On that plain he made out the gleaming vastness of a city that made New York a village.

46

"There it is," said Edri. "The hub and center of the galaxy."

Trehearne only shook his head. By this time he had no words. He watched the boundaries of the city widen, he watched the towers of its buildings lift and rise until they seemed to bear the sky upon them, and he was silent. Still dropping, but slowly now in a soundless glide, the ship bore to the southward. Here for miles the spaceport ran, the great docks that cradled the giants of the stars. Here was an ordered, ceaseless, swarming chaos of men and machines, seen from Trehearne's position now as a sort of yeasty ferment lapping around and over the apparently endless rows of titanic docks. The sheer size of it was crushing.

The warning bells rang. Trehearne came partly out of his daze and went below with the others to await the landing. Seconds ticked by, and the blood was hammering in his temples, and his muscles twitched with a nervous excitement. Landing. Landing on a strange world, under a strange new sun . . .

Smoothly, softly, the great keel touched down, home again from the edges of the universe.

Trehearne stood up. The others were already moving, pouring into the corridor, laughing, talking, eager for the opened lock and home. Trehearne would have followed them, but Edri's hand was on him, and Kerrel was in front of him.

"You'll wait," said Kerrel. "Edri, you're responsible for him. See that he doesn't leave the ship."

He went out, and suddenly, for Trehearne, that keen fine edge of wonder was all gone. Shairn came up and gave him a reassuring smile. "Don't worry, Michael. Old Joris is a friend of mine." She went out, too, and Trehearne said to Edri, "Who is Joris?"

"The Coordinator of the Port. In his younger days he flew for Shairn's father." Edri sank down into a chair again. "Might as well take it easy. Kerrel's gone to make his report to Joris in person. This isn't the sort of thing you want too widely broadcast."

"Why Joris? I thought Kerrel worked for the Council."

"He does. But everything that goes in or out of this

47

port has to clear through the Coordinator's office. Sit down, Trehearne, you make me nervous."

"Do you think she'll be able to do anything?"

"I hope so. Damn it, sit down!"

He sat. There were noises in the ship, but they were unfamiliar ones, the impersonal clangings and boomings of freight hatches, machinery, the invading boots and unknown voices of dockside men. The sounds of the port outside came to him muffled and subdued, like the ceaseless roll of thunder a long way off. There was a feeling of cessation. The voyage was over. Out there a new sun was shining, there was air unbreathed by any man of Earth and a whole wide world waiting, a Vardda world, his as much as theirs, but he was barred from it, he was kept under hatches like a criminal, unable even to speak while strangers decided his fate. It scared him, and it angered him, and the more he felt trapped and helpless the more furious he got. His body would not stay still. He sprang up and began to stride the floor, and Edri watched him speculatively.

"Get good and mad," he said. "You can't fight unless you're mad."

"I'll fight."

"You know the line to take. Don't be afraid to let 'em have it."

"I won't."

Time passed. Edri sat and smoked. Trehearne paced, sat down, and paced again. A year went by, and then another, and then a young man, very brisk, very efficient, very self-assured, came in and looked at them.

"You're to come to the Coordinator's office," he said, and stared with frank curiosity at Trehearne. Then he turned to Edri. "He *looks* all right. Is this story really true?"

"Never mind," said Edri. "Come on, Trehearne."

He followed them, down the long corridor and into the lock chamber, leaving the ship as he had first entered it so long ago, so far away. He stepped out onto the open dock, and the full roaring, thundering impact of the biggest spaceport in the galaxy hit him like an explosion.

Row upon row, and on all sides, the towering docks stretched to the end of his seeing and beyond. Ships lay in most of them, recumbent monsters taking their ease, while men and machines in vast numbers and great complexity waited on their needs. The ringing air was heavy with smells, strange spices and subtle unidentifiable things mingling with the reek of oil and hot metal, cargoes of unimagined riches from unimaginable worlds. Trehearne stood, feeling the tremendous pulse beat through him, hardly aware for the moment that Edri was trying to steer him to a kiosk at the end of the dock, or that the young Vardda was amused at his wide-eyed astonishment.

In endless hordes, men swarmed upon the looming hulls and went busily along the docks, testing, checking, guiding and managing the machines. They were not Vardda men. They were men from the other worlds, who could not fly the stars. A lot of them—and here Trehearne's eyes opened even wider, because even though he had been told, seeing is another thing—were not at all what he would have called human. But in spite of their strangeness, they seemed familiar. They were like any of the cheerful, hard-handed, competent men to be seen around any port of Earth, serving the ships and the planes. The incessant noise was deafening. Gigantic cranes moved ponderously on their tracks, shifting cargoes between strings of carriers and the gaping holds. Small trams weaved in and out of the confusion. At intervals between the docks were lines of shops, where atomic-powered forges shaped new parts, new plates and housings. Here a crew worked on a hull with flaring welders, and there a great bow section was lowered slowly into place with an ear-shattering clang.

Edri's voice reached him, thin and faint. "Big business, Trehearne. The biggest in the galaxy. Impressive, isn't it?"

He urged Trehearne along, toward the kiosk that was still some way ahead. They walked in a railed-off path, and in a moment Trehearne saw coming toward them on the other side of the rail a large and very involved piece of machinery that seemed to be walking slowly the length of the ship's hull, guided by one small human attendant and bearing in its belly another one who sat surrounded by dials and counters and little screens.

"That's an X-ray scanner," Edri told him. "They get

49

first crack at every ship that lands. These ultra speeds have effects on metals in time. The scanners test the structure of the metals for crystallization, or any abnormal molecular shift. The ships become unsafe after a certain period of service—usually a fairly long one—and they're watched very closely. It's no fun having a hull fall apart on you in the middle of nowhere."

He pushed Trehearne on, into the kiosk. The young Vardda was still amused. Edri said, "There's a lift here. We go down."

Trehearne stepped in, and turned. Just before the door closed smoothly in his face, he caught a glimpse of a tall white pylon in the distance, dominating the whole field, and knew without being told that it housed Port Administration and his immediate destiny. Once more the sense of wonder was stripped away. The lift dropped and his heart dropped with it, swiftly down.

The trip was short. The lift set them in a passageway far underground, and the passageway led to a tube, all very quiet after the roaring of the port. A small monorail car took them in a handful of minutes to the levels underneath the pylon, and then there was another lift, a private one this time, going up. There was a bitter taste in Trehearne's mouth, and the palms of his hands were sweating.

He thought the lift would never stop, but it did, on the highest level. The brisk young man motioned them out, and there was an office, bare and spacious, with window walls that looked on all sides across the spaceport. Trehearne thought fleetingly that it was less like an office than the bridge of a starship, pathetically shackled to the soil.

Shairn was there, and Kerrel, standing far apart and very stiff, their faces set and stubborn. Kerrel did not turn, but Shairn came to Trehearne and took his hand defiantly. Off at one side a second brisk young man presided over some sort of a recording device. There seemed to be a good deal of silence in the place, brought on, perhaps, by the arrival of the lift, for no one was in a silent mood—least of all the man who faced them from the other side of a massive table. Trehearne saw a grizzled, heavy-shouldered giant who was never designed to occupy an office. The walls cramped him, even such walls as these, because they were bounded by horizons. His large scarred hands rested uneasily on the polished wood, impatient of the papers that were stacked there, and his eyes seemed better used to watching stars than men. Those eyes, pale blue as winter ice, sought out Trehearne and did not waver until they had cut from him every bit of knowledge to be had.

"I didn't believe it," Joris said, "but I can see now why you didn't like the idea of killing him. Too much like one of us. But damn it!—Kerrel, you of all people should have remembered the law. No non-Vardda personnel under any circumstances to board any craft designed for interstellar flight. What got into you?"

Before Kerrel could answer, Shairn spoke for him. "A certain squeamishness," she said, "and a doubt. I think he regrets them both, now. You see, Joris, there *was* a legal doubt. Looking at Trehearne, could you tell he was non-Vardda?"

"But you knew it. . . ."

"Oh no," said Edri pointedly, "we didn't. We didn't know at all until he survived the take-off, and then he couldn't very well be classified as non-Vardda—could he, Joris?"

Joris moved his huge bulk uncomfortably. "A freak," he said . "A mongrel. You didn't do him any kindness to bring him here. Shairn, I get a feeling that you had a hand in this. In fact, knowing you . . ."

Shairn snapped, "What I do is my own business. And as for Michael, he's as good a Vardda as you are. You haven't answered my question yet. Will you let him stay in my custody until the Council meets?"

"No! And that's final."

"But Joris . . ."

"You're a trouble-maker, Shairn. You have been since the day you were born. But I'm damned if you'll make trouble for me!"

"And I thought you were my friend, Joris, you ought to remember . . ."

"I took orders from your father when I flew his ships, but you're not the man he was! And furthermore, I'm not working for you now, I'm working for the government. Is that clear?"

"Perfectly." She added, in a tone of admiration, "Anyway, you haven't forgotten how to roar."

Surprisingly, Joris laughed. "No," he said, "no more than you've learned manners." He glanced from Shairn to the stony-faced Kerrel, who was still standing like a ramrod and saying nothing—Trehearne gathered that he had already said everything he considered necessary—and then back to Edri and the Earthman. "I'll admit this is one hell of a queer mess, and I'm glad I don't have to decide the final outcome. As I see it, my duty now is to keep him in custody like any other undesirable, until the Council takes him off my hands." He looked hard at Shairn. "That's the law, and that's the way it's going to be."

Kerrel spoke at last. "Good. That's what I wanted to be sure of."

Joris glowered at him. "I'm considered fairly reliable in the performance of my office." He nodded to the brisk young man who had brought Trehearne and Edri from the ship. "Make out the usual interim commitment form for suspected persons under the Port Authority Code, Section C . . ."

Trehearne said, "Just a minute." He stepped forward until he was facing Joris across the table. "You have no authority to imprison me."

Joris stared at him. Then he shook his head irritably as though he thought his ears must be playing him tricks, and stared again. His jowls took on a tinge of red. Trehearne went on. The time had come to let his temper go, and he turned it loose of all restraint.

"Unless he is formally accused of a crime, no Vardda may be detained by anyone against his will. I have committed no crime, and I have not been accused of any."

It took Joris some time to recover his voice. When he did , it fairly rattled the windows. "You are *not* a Vardda!"

"No? Think a minute. What is the one distinguishing quality of a Vardda that marks him as different from all other men?"

"All right, I'll answer that! By some freak or other you managed to survive the flight. But that doesn't change the fact that you're an Earthman, born and bred, and therefore not a Vardda!"

Trehearne's eyes had acquired a hard glitter. "Then suppose," he said, "that you imprison me—an Earthman who has crossed the galaxy from Sol to Aldebaran, and lived. That'll make quite an uproar, won't it? All the non-Vardda peoples will be much interested. So will the Orthist party. I don't doubt they'll spread the news all over the galaxy—*the Vardda have admitted that they're not the only ones who can fly interstellar space!*"

Shairn said, "That's it, Michael! Go it!" Edri had drawn back a little. His eyes were sober and intent. Kerrel spoke, and his voice was sharp. "You've had bad advice, Trehearne. That kind of talk won't help you."

Joris motioned him to silence. To Trehearne he said, "What do you know about the Orthist party?"

"Enough to know that they could make a great deal of trouble. Either I'm Vardda or I'm not. And if I'm not, I could be the start of a whole new movement. The first non-Vardda to fly the stars, the first crack in the monopoly."

Joris shook his head. "You can be put away so quickly and quietly that no one will ever hear of you."

"Good," said Trehearne. "Put me away. Put away all the officers of the ship. Put away all the passengers. Put away all the crew. There's a lot of people to keep quiet."

Shairn broke in triumphantly. "Yes, Joris! How are you going to silence me?"

"And," said Edri, "me."

Joris looked from one to the other and back again, his brows drawn angrily together. But he said nothing. Kerrel leaned over the table.

"Joris," he said, "do you understand? The man is trying to blackmail you with an open threat of treason."

"Yes," said Trehearne, "I am." His voice was suddenly very quiet, and he spoke straight to Joris. "When I made that flight and lived I won my right to the freedom of the stars. I won my right to fly deep space, and I will use any weapons I can get my hands on against any man who tries to keep me from it."

Then, for quite a long while, no one spoke.

"By God," said Joris slowly, "I take it back. There can't be any mongrel blood in you. Only a Vardda could have that kind of insolence." He got up and came round

53

the table. "You, Shairn. In spite of your political views, you'll back him up in this?"

"I will. And it's probably the only real accomplishment the Orthists will ever make."

"And you, Edri?"

"All the way."

Kerrel swore. It was the first time Trehearne had ever heard him do it, and it was aimed directly at Shairn. "For God's sake, watch what you're saying! Joris, she doesn't mean it, and she won't do it. I know her feelings on the subject too well for that."

Shairn said, "Try me."

Joris had become very thoughtful. "You know," he said to Kerrel, "whether she does or not, there's a great deal of truth in what the Earthman says. Far too much, I'm afraid, to be overlooked."

"Bluff," said Kerrel. "Look here, Joris, if you turn this man loose, I'll have to report . . ."

"Oh, report and be damned! The law says I have to shut him up, and shut him up I will, and there my duty ends. And I don't need you to tell me my business." He went to the recorder, took out the spool, dropped it on the floor and crushed it under his boot. "Now clear out, all of you. Dismissed. And I'd advise you all to keep your mouths shut. Especially *you*," he said to the two very young men. "You have enough work to keep you busy. Go and do it. You stay here, Trehearne."

Trehearne stayed and there was a bitter thought in him that he had failed. The faces of the others, as they left, were full of doubt. Presently he was alone with Joris in the sweep of golden light from the windows. From the eastern quadrant of the port Trehearne saw a great ship rise and clear away for distant suns.

Joris walked the floor, and said nothing. The silence was heavy, an oppressive thing. It was not touched by the sounds of the port, so far below. They were outside it, and the face of Joris was a heavy, sombre mask. Trehearne looked out at the alien sky, where the clouds burned like little nebulae, and then down again at the ships. From this vantage he could see the sector where the planetary craft came in, the slow freighters from the non-Vardda worlds of Aldebaran, and it came to him suddenly how the poor bastards that flew them must feel, watching the starships come and go and knowing they could never follow. Beyond the port the towers of the city rose, and Trehearne wondered if he would ever see it.

Joris stopped his pacing and said, "Come here."

Trehearne obeyed. The pale eyes, harsh and keen as an old eagle's, probed into him, weighing, judging. Trehearne stood and waited. He said nothing. There was nothing more to say.

"Vardda blood," Joris muttered to himself. "Unmistakable. And he wants to fly the stars." He asked abruptly, "Were you a foundling?"

"No," said Trehearne. And then he added slowly, "But I might just as well have been."

Joris turned away, his brows drawn and brooding, his head and shoulders massive against the background of the burning sky. "How old are you?"

"Thirty-three, in Earth years."

Still with his back to Trehearne, Joris spoke. "I think I see a way. Whether it will work or not, I don't know. The Council convenes again in five days, at which time I'll be required to make my report on you, and I'll do what I can. Meanwhile, you'll have to go where I tell you and stay there without any fuss. Is that clear?"

"Yes." The pulse of hope had begun to beat again.

"Good. And Trehearne—"

"Yes?"

"If things turn out all right, you *will* fly the stars!"

It was a threat as much as a promise.

Thirty minutes later, after a journey under guard in a sublevel tubecar that left him in complete ignorance of his whereabouts, Trehearne was conducted into a square neat cubicle, comfortable in all respects but none the less a prison cell. The magnetic lock clicked behind him and he was alone.

There were no windows. He did not even know whether he was above or below ground. There was neither day nor night nor time. He paced the narrow floor and ate the unfamiliar food delivered to him automatically through a slot in the wall, and tried to sleep. He smoked the last of his hoarded cigarettes and thought of Earth and the distances between the suns. He hoped and hope became gradually a grim despair.

55

No one came. Shairn had forgotten him. Edri's friendship had turned feeble at the last. The trap that Joris had set for him became more obvious with each passing hour. He hated them all. He raged and waited and remembered the old man's words—*You can be put away so quickly and quietly that no one will ever hear of you.*

This was his landing on Llyrdis, the fruit of his journey across the star-shot universe. This was the end of his dream.

He ceased to rage.

There came a time when he awoke sharply from uneasy sleep to hear the low click of the lock and a soft slurred step on the floor, coming toward him. He sprang up, and saw that it was Shairn. She cried out, *"Michael!"* and her words came to him with a sound of unreality, like the voices heard through fever.

"It's all over, Michael—and you're free!"

IX

AN HOUR HAD GONE BY AND HE STILL COULD NOT QUITE believe it. He had left the cell behind him and the five eternal days of waiting. He stood on a terrace high above the city. It was night, and the burning moons were brilliant in the sky. The wind from the sea had the clean sting of wine, but it was not like the sea winds he remembered, it was new and strange, intensely thrilling. Around him the tall slim towers rose upward toward the moons, and far below the shining web of streets was a pattern of sensual beauty, many-colored, sounding, alive.

Shairn said softly, "Look at it, Michael. It's all yours."

He looked. His hands were tight on the terrace rail,

and there was a fullness in him that made it hard to breathe.

"I had something to do with it, Michael. Aren't you going to thank me?"

He turned. She had put on a flowing thing of white, cunningly draped and spangled over with a diamond frost, and there were strange jewels caught in the dark masses of her hair. He started to speak and then forgot the words, when sounds from inside the apartment—it was Edri's—announced the arrival of Joris.

"Come now, and hear how the miracle was done."

From the terrace they passed through sliding doors of glass, open now to the warm breeze, into a low, broad, spacious room of the utmost simplicity and comfort. A millionaire's room, Trehearne would have said, and yet Edri was a poor man by Vardda standards, owning no ships and working for those who did. The window walls looked out over the city, a mighty panorama of light and color that was without garishness, and inside there was quiet and homeliness, made personal by the small things Edri had brought home from his voyages. Robots of various sorts did all the cleaning automatically when he was away, and there was no kitchen. Meals arrived by pressure tube, fresh, hot, and to order, from a service center. Remembering his own bachelor quarters on Earth, Trehearne was overcome with envy.

Joris came toward him, holding out a huge hard hand. Trehearne shook it, and Joris said, "What were you thinking, those five days in the cell?"

Trehearne shook his head. "I won't tell you, since none of it was true."

Joris laughed. Edri said, "We haven't told him anything. We left that for you." He found glasses and poured wine. Joris settled heavily into a chair, full of an honest pride in his own cleverness, beaming with it. Shairn curled up near him on a wide couch and sipped her wine. "Go on," she said. "We're waiting."

"It took a lot of juggling," Joris said, "and more than a little downright forgery, but it worked. You see, Trehearne, a full record of all voyages is kept at Port administration. I went back between thirty and forty years and managed to supply you with a pretty good background." He leaned forward. "You get this into your

57

head, and keep it there. You were born on Earth thirty-four years ago of Vardda parents then engaged in trading activities on that planet. Your mother died in childbirth and your father was forced to abandon you, since even a Vardda infant cannot endure interstellar flight. The people who brought you up, and whom you had assumed to be your own parents, merely fostered you." He paused, searching through his trouser pockets until he found a slip of paper, which he handed to Trehearne. "Here are the names of your real parents. Memorize them. Your father has since been killed in a wreck off Orion Nebula and you have no brothers or sisters. Incidentally, you have no inheritance either, since according to law your father's estate was divided upon his death. From now on, this is your only history. Don't forget it. And don't talk about any of it more than you're forced to."

Trehearne stared at the paper and the two names that were written there. "I didn't think it could be done—But what did Kerrel say about this? He surely didn't believe the story."

"He couldn't prove it wasn't so. And I produced such convincing records that the evidence was overwhelming." He laughed. "Matter of fact, I cut the ground right out from under him."

"He didn't like it," Shairn said. "But there was nothing he could do, and there never will be anything he can do. Joris and I managed to persuade the Council not to have you appear for questioning, Michael—on the very good grounds that the less said about it the better. The hearing was closed, with the news services barred out. Joris' records, and your Vardda characteristics were sufficiently convincing. They passed their resolution in less than thirty minutes, and then followed it by another to tighten the laws against Vardda children being born on any world but Llyrdis!"

Trehearne put the piece of paper in his pocket. "There's a lot of things I want to say, but—" He broke off, and Edri shoved a glass in his hand. "Don't try," he said. "Just tell us honestly that we're wonderful, and we'll be satisfied. Incidentally, don't ever make me out a liar. I reported the most interesting statements from you concerning your unhappy childhood as a foundling."

Trehearne grinned. He looked from one to the other, and finally his gaze centered on Joris. "There's one thing I don't understand. Why did you do this for me?"

"Don't ever question a man's reasons, as long as they're good, Trehearne. And now you're a Vardda, stamped and sealed, you've got another problem ahead of you. You have to make a living. Do you still want to fly the stars?" He saw the look on Trehearne's face and smiled. "I need a supercargo on my ship *Saarga*, outbound in two weeks for trade in the Hercules cluster. Officers and crew fly on shares and it's a rich voyage. Even a supercargo should do well."

Edri said, "I ought to warn you, Trehearne. The Hercules run is one of the toughest in the galaxy."

"That's why it pays so well," said Joris. "Well?"

Before Trehearne could answer, Shairn laid her hand lazily on his shoulder and said, "Nonsense, Joris. He doesn't have to take on anything like that. I can find a better opening in my fleet and he won't starve until I do."

Trehearne's face tightened. He said quietly, "I seem to have heard, Shairn, that you're quite well off."

"Oh, quite! Thirty ships to Joris' two. My father was smart, and I was lucky enough to be his only heir. Oh, the devil with it—who wants to talk business! Come on, Michael, we'll show you the city."

"In a minute." Joris was looking at him with an odd expression, and Trehearne's mouth tightened another notch. He said, "When shall I report aboard the *Saarga?*"

Edri leaned over Shairn's shoulder and whispered, "I think you've got our Michael angry."

Joris looked at Shairn and roared. "Missed your guess, didn't you?" He got up. "All right, Trehearne, I'll let you know. And now let's see what we can do in the way of a celebration!"

They went. But for the next hour or so Shairn was inclined to be sulky, and was all the more so because Trehearne seemed to have forgotten her existence.

Resplendent in black and silver supplied for him out of Edri's wardrobe, free, accepted, and with a future ahead, Trehearne walked the streets of the city, drunk with color and sound and movement, dazed with the incredible size and the utter strangeness of the greatest metropolis in the galaxy. It surged magnificently, crowded, thriving, beautiful, drenched in the wealth and inventiveness of a thousand far-flung cultures, Mecca for all the peoples of Aldebaran's seven inhabited planets. And its beauty was honest. There were no dark and evil places hidden behind the splendid buildings, no slums, no poverty, no ugliness. The Vardda had travelled widely, and seen much, and they had learned from others. From a vantage point given to no other people in history, they had studied and compared the inceptions, growths, and collapses of more empires, races, and cultures than a man could count in a year, and the work still went on under the direction of their best minds, correlating and compiling, examining causes and evolving from the mass of evidence ways and means to keep the Vardda empire healthy. They had managed well for a thousand years, and Trehearne felt a tremendous admiration for them, laboring as they did under the extra handicap of an essentially inbred society. Their government was elective, and they kept it clean. Their laws were relatively few and simple, and they were obeyed. They oppressed nobody, and saw to it that their non-Vardda neighbors benefited heavily from the Vardda trade.

"It's not at all," Edri had told him once, "that we're so much more bloody noble than anybody else. Matter of fact, we're probably unrivalled in our basic selfishness. It's good business, you see. Keep everybody as happy as possible, deal as fairly as you can, make 'em all rich, and you don't have trouble, which is bad for trade. The non-Vardda races may not love us, but they're not inclined to try getting along without us. As for domestic politics and administration, it's simple self-preservation to keep them sound. We're not utopians, to use one of your favorite Earthly terms, we just try to make sense."

Looking at the city, Trehearne thought they had done a remarkably good job. Actually, few of the Vardda were urbanites. Llyrdis was essentially a world of estates and small communities. The Vardda sociologists had not been blind to that final corrosive stage of civilization that Spengler called Megalopolis. The city was not a place in which great mobs of people spent their lives. It was a clearing house, a warehouse, an office, a factory, devoted entirely to business. The population was chiefly non-Vardda, and they only stayed there during their employment. Their homes were on their own worlds. They inhabited the city without being trapped in it.

As for Trehearne, it seemed to him that night that he could spend a lifetime there and never tire of it. The little ships that tramped the narrow planetary roads set down beside the scornful giants of the star-trails and poured into the metropolis a never-ending tide of visitors, come to touch the fringes of a glory they could never grasp thenselves, to revel in alien pleasures and barter for the gems and spices and the spider-woven silks of worlds that they would never see. Most of them were human or nearly so, their skins a variety of tints, their costumes outlandish or sober according to their native custom. Some were not human at all, except in intelligence and pride of bearing.

"See those black-skinned, hawk-nosed chaps with the bronze wings?" Edri's hand guided Trehearne's wondering gaze. "They're from Suumis. And the three silvery ones over there with the bright crests and the crimson robes. They're the dominant race on the second world sunward, and proud as Lucifer for all they've got scales instead of skin. That little bluish fellow is a merchant-prince from Zaard, the outermost planet. See his diamond caste-mark?"

Trehearne saw. He mazed his brain with seeing, with hearing and feeling—the pulse and rush of the city, the kaleidoscopic multitudes, the companies of lordly Vardda like peacocks in their jewels and brilliant tunics, the babel of outworld tongues, the drifting sound of music, strange and sweet. From place to place the four of them drifted, in no hurry, wandering as the mood took them, drinking the dark wine of Antares, the pungent snow-white brew of Fomalhaut, endless wines of many colors from the worlds of many stars. Shairn forgot to sulk. To Trehearne she seemed to float in moonlight and laughter, bewitching and unattainable as a creature seen in dreams. The wine mounted to his head. The excitement, the strangeness, the wild joy of release put a kind of fever in him, and his surroundings lost reality, whirling ever faster and in brighter colors round him, visions

61

painted on a blowing mist. Faces, human, half-human, unhuman, beautiful, grotesque, ludicrous. Carnival masks, reeling, dancing. Vardda women lovely as sin, dressed in a thousand fashions from a thousand worlds, smiling with red mouths. Music throbbing, beating, wailing, unknown melodies plucked from unknown strings, passionate, soft, mingling with the smell of wine and perfume and the sharp sea wind. Dancing girls with emerald skins, outlandish beasts that capered with an eerie cleverness, a spinning whirl of pleasure-palaces, terraces, gardens, parks and squares, nameless trees blowing under the triple moons, Shairn's laughing face, Joris flushed and jovial, a grey-polled ox on holiday, Edri . . .

There was something wrong with Edri. Perhaps the wine had given Trehearne a sharper insight, or perhaps it was only that the outside stimuli had grown so bewildering that he fled from them at last, unconsciously, by turning to the familiar as personified by his friends. At any rate, he emerged a little from his daze and realized that while he and Shairn and Joris had been growing gayer Edri had grown steadily more solemn and withdrawn. Sobriety was not habitual with him, but Trehearne had never seen him really drunk. He was drunk now, and he was continuing to drink as though there was not enough wine on Llyrdis to fill him, sitting silently, his eyes fixed on some inner distance, a brooding look on his ugly face. Trehearne spoke to him, and he answered, but it was only a mechanical reflex, a sound without meaning.

They were in a place of trees and crystal columns, with bowers drowned in bloom and the open sky above. Trehearne looked at the others. They were happy, without a care in the world. Then he saw Edri's face again, bleak and sad and seeing nothing, and he frowned. He was fond of Edri. It came over him in a rush how fond he was of him. He leaned forward and said, "What is it, Edri? What's wrong?"

"He's sober," Joris said. "He needs more wine." He reached over and poured a ruby liquid into Edri's glass. Abruptly Edri shook his head and pushed the goblet away. He was looking now at something behind Trehearne. "No," he said. "I'm going home."

"There's no hurry, Edri. Stay a while." It was Kerrel's voice. Startled, Trehearne turned his head and saw him standing there, as though he had been standing for a long time. Now he came forward and sat down with them. Trehearne could not tell what he was thinking. He did not like a man whose thoughts he could not even guess at.

"Congratulations," Kerrel said. "I don't believe a word of it, of course, but that history of Trehearne was a fine piece of strategy."

Joris laughed. "The Council believed it. Furthermore, I believe it, Shairn believes it—even Trehearne believes it, don't you, Trehearne?"

"Of course."

"Well, it's done now," Kerrel said, as though it had ceased to matter.

Shairn picked up one of the musky flowers and tossed it into Kerrel's lap. "Have you forgotten me?" she asked him, with a curious edged sweetness. "I know you. You're a bad loser, and it's no use pretending you're not. Besides, I've seen you this way before. Just what are you meditating in your little mind?"

"Nothing at all, but the usual broad speculations on life. Curious what twists and turns it has. Take today. One man escapes banishment and another, a respected member of our community, incurs it."

"Who?" said Joris, peering sharply at Kerrel as through a fog.

"Arrin."

There was a small silence. Then Shairn said, "But I met him once. He's nice. You can't send him to Thuvis."

"I'm afraid there's no doubt about it. He's one of the Orthist leaders—you didn't know that, did you?" His question was addressed to no one in particular. "We've suspected him for some time, and today he was caught. Odd thing, though. They couldn't find any of his papers." He turned casually to Edri. "Arrin's a friend of yours, isn't he?"

"I know him."

"Oh, come now! You've known him for years."

Edri said nastily, "I've known you for a long time

too. Don't cat-and-mouse with me, Kerrel. If you have something to say, say it."

Kerrel shrugged. "I was only thinking that a man can have too many unfortunate friendships."

"Does that include me?" said Trehearne, getting up.

"Oh, the hell with him," said Edri. He lurched to his feet, giving Kerrel one smouldering look, but it was Trehearne he spoke to. "He's a tireless and worthy investigator, a good cop as you would say on Earth. But he enjoys his work too much. I'm leaving."

He walked away, staggering a bit but holding himself rigidly erect. Trehearne watched the solitary figure moving down an avenue of trees, splashed with shadows and golden light. He hesitated, and then followed.

Edri stopped when he felt Trehearne's hand touch him. He looked at him in a curious way, almost as though he had never seen him before. And now that he was here, Trehearne did not know what to say. Rather awkwardly, he asked, "Can I do anything?"

"No. Thanks."

"I'm sorry about your friend."

"Why should you be? He's an Orthist, a traitor. He deserves to be sent to Thuvis."

Remembering the desolate picture he had seen of that world at the end of the galaxy, and his own so narrow escape from it, Trehearne shivered. "I don't care. It doesn't seem right to send anybody to rot forever in that boneyard. Besides, I can't see that the Orthists are so bad."

Edri reached out and took hold of Trehearne's shoulders. "Hate them," he said earnestly. "Hate them with everything you've got."

He turned away, and Trehearne said with a certain exasperation, "Hate 'em or not, I don't see why they're such a danger."

"There was a message, Trehearne. Long after Orthis disappeared, one of the life-skiffs of his ship was picked up in space. There was nothing in it but a message, painted in big letters on the walls. It was addressed to his enemies, and it said, 'You have not destroyed me. The peoples of the Galaxy will yet be given the freedom of the stars.' You understand? There was still hope, from the Orthist point of view."

He went on, a drunken man, not talking to Trehearne now but to himself, to the wind and the casual moons and a world that had turned bitter around him "Arrin worked. All his life he worked, like a lot of men before him. He searched the records, the closed files that nobody is allowed to look at, and then they caught him. He never found what he was looking for, but he might have. A little more time, and he might have!" He looked up into the sky, the empty sky that stretched away to the rim of the universe. "Somewhere out there Orthis sits in his ship and waits—waits to be found again. But where? That's it, the question no one has answered in a thousand years. Where?"

He turned aside and was abruptly, violently sick. Trehearne waited. Afterward Edri muttered, "It's curious, the things a man will say when he's drunk."

"I don't know," Trehearne said. "I didn't hear anything."

"Don't ever hear anything, for your sake as well as mine." He mananged a smile. "Thanks. I'm all right now. I'm going on home."

He walked away slowly, and Trehearne went back to the others. He had sobered up a bit himself, and some of the magic had gone out of the evening. He was worried about Edri.

Shairn looked up at him, heavy-eyed. "You were gone so long, Michael."

"Holding Edri's head." Kerrel was still there. A sour mood seemed to have come over everyone. Joris sat with his head hanging forward. His eyes were open, staring moodily into the spilled wine, but he was obviously on the verge of passing out. Shairn had torn to bits the pale flowers in her lap, scattering them on the grass. No one was talking. Kerrel had not touched the wine. He was looking at Shairn, just sitting still and looking at her. Trehearne said to him, "You haven't given en up, have you?"

"No."

"He only thinks he hasn't," Shairn said angrily. She rose and stood in front of Kerrel. "What is it you just can't bear to give up—me, or my thirty ships?"

Kerrel got up. He lifted his hand and slapped her hard across the cheek. There was a second when no one moved, when Shairn's eyes blazed wider and wider, and then Trehearne thrust her aside and moved in. Kerrel was stony sober and his reflexes were fast. The next thing Trehearne saw, through a ringing haze, was Kerrel walking away, leaving small sharp scars in the turf where his heels had cut in.

"No," said Shairn. "Not this time, Michael. Let him go."

His head hurt. The wine was turning on him, and he felt ashamed. He wanted to kill Kerrel, and he couldn't.

Shairn said uneasily, "I'm not mad. That's funny, Michael. I'm not mad at all, I'm scared."

"Why?"

"Him." She nodded after the dark figure receding among the trees.

"He'd never hurt you."

"Not directly. It's you I'm thinking of. He won't let you go. He was warning me. He can't let you go, and it isn't only because of me, or his pride. I've left him before, but this is different. You're different. He knows we lied to the Council."

"What can he do?"

"You saw him go after Edri. I don't know, Michael, but be careful. Don't give him even the hint of a chance at you." She shook her head. "I've changed my mind. I'm glad you're going voyaging. And meanwhile, you'd better not see much of Edri."

"You love me, Shairn?"

"I should think I'd done enough to prove it!"

"Don't get your back up. I was only wondering. Would you really have gone to the Orthists to help me?"

She laughed. "It was a safe threat to make. I knew Joris would never call it."

As though the sound of his name had decided him, Joris fell quietly sideways and began to snore. Trehearne bent over him, and he thought he saw in the moonlight a curious thing. He thought he saw tears on the old man's cheeks. He decided he must be very drunk indeed.

Shairn touched his arm. "Come, Michael."

"Where?"

"The home of my family, the Silver Tower. There's so little time to be happy in, before you go."

Two weeks later, dressed in the black and scarlet of the Vardda spacemen, Trehearne left Llyrdis behind him for the starship *Saarga*, outbound for Hercules.

X

THE "SAARGA" WAS NOT LIKE THE SHIP THAT HAD brought Trehearne from Earth. She was older and shabbier and clumsier, a great lumbering beldame of a ship with enormous capacity for cargo and no space at all for passengers. Officers and crew were cramped into quarters functionally reduced to the absolute minimum, and there were no such luxuries as lounges and observation domes. But to Trehearne she was a thing of beauty, of miracle and wonder. Every dent and scar on her unlovely bulkheads recorded a voyage to a nameless sun. The crammed and odorous vaults of her belly were storehouses of exotic riches. She was outbound for Hercules, and he was part of her. He was no longer merely a hungry onlooker. He belonged. He worshipped her.

He saw her first lying hugely in the dock, her scored and pitted hull-plates giving back a dull glint from the sun. He looked up at her, and then around him at the tremendous clamor of the port, and then he strode down along the walkway feeling ten feet high and happy as a kid at a carnival. He reported aboard, was duly checked in and assigned to quarters in a very small cabin with four very narrow bunks, where he good-naturedly allowed himself to be elbowed into the least desirable upper. His cabin-mates were all younger than he, but they were veterans, and he was forced to admit that this was his first professional voyage.

"Trehearne," said the dark-haired youngster in Lower Two, turning the name over on his tongue and frowning. "Funny sort of name—I've heard it somewhere."

The copper-haired youngster—the youngest—in Upper One, said, "I know. My uncle was talking about him. He's the fellow they found on Earth. Aren't you, Trehearne?"

"Yes."

The dark-haired youngster whistled. "Were you in luck! It was a million-to-one chance you'd ever even meet another Vardda. What's it like on Earth? I've never been there."

"It's all right," Trehearne said, "for Earthmen."

The first of the warning bells rang for take-off. They settled themselves in the padded bunks, and the long, lean, cheerful-looking man in Lower One, whose youth was already overlaid with many kinds of experience, glanced up at Trehearne and said, "You're not used to this, are you?"

"No." Trehearne's belly had contracted suddenly into a hard knot, and his skin was cold with a clammy sweat. The agonies of that first take-off returned to him full force. He knew this one would not be as bad. Once the adjustment was made, you were all right. Everybody said so. It didn't make any difference. He was scared.

The man in Lower One said quietly, "Just take it easy. By the way, my name is Yann. Radar crew."

"Hello."

The second warning sounded. Trehearne's teeth shut together with a snap and his jaw muscles stood out in ridges.

Red-head in Upper One said, "I'm Perri. Low man in the generator room."

Trehearne grunted.

The voice of Lower Two, directly beneath him, said, "If you fall through, I'll catch you. I'm Astrogation-Computer Technician, Second Class. A big mouth-filling title, but all I do is punch keys. They call me Rohan."

Trehearne said painfully, "On Earth there was a Cardinal. . . ."

68

Third warning. Silence. A drawing-in, a throb, a quiver, and then a leap . . .

"Trehearne? Trehearne, are you still there?"

"Yes—" *Crushed, weighted, stupefied, but it isn't so bad, it isn't nearly so bad, not much worse than pulling out of a dive. And she's going up, oh God she's going up!*

The air-shriek died. The soundlessness of space was wrapped around the hull outside, and within there was the soft and mighty beating of that pulse that Trehearne remembered, going faster, going higher. A sigh escaped him, and his body relaxed. He smiled. He was where he wanted to be.

The long haul out to Hercules was uneventful, and the others found it dull. But for Trehearne, every minute of it was charged with magic. He was called up once before the skipper, who looked hard at him and said, "Joris told me to see that you worked. There's more to being a starman than lounging around in your bunk, and you'll be wanting to take examinations for some kind of a rating sooner or later. Here, study these. And in your spare time, learn all you can about the ship."

"These" proved to be texts on the Vardda Trade Laws, manuals on the rules and regulations governing relations with other races, and a history in many microvolumes of the trans-galactic expansion of the Vardda race in its thousand years of existence. He knew that Joris must have supplied the books and he was glad to get them. The trade codes, like laws anywhere, were pretty dull stuff and interesting only because of the fantastically broad field they dealt with. The manuals were better, because they were full of references to alien and frequently non-human races, with fascinating glimpses into the damndest customs and psychologies Trehearne had ever heard of. But the history held him spellbound.

It began with a foreword on what the Vardda had been like in the millenniums before Orthis, when they were simply the people of Llyrdis. It seemed to Trehearne that they were not too different from the people of Earth. They had had their ages of barbarism and change and growth, and their homogeneity had not been achieved without pain. However, they had achieved it,

69

and at an earlier period in their world-culture than that in which his native planet now was. He thought perhaps the task had been easier for the Llyrdians because there were fewer geographic barriers to the free mingling of peoples in their nomadic phase. The oceans were land-locked and the mountain ranges were broken by travers-able passes. No primitive tribe had grown to statehood in even partial isolation, and the cultural streams had flowed strongly in all directions, losing their narrow in-tensity and broadening out into what eventually became one universal lake. It made for dulness in the world pic-ture, perhaps, because of a sameness in dress and lan-guage and custom, but it was steady, and it led to a con-ception of the individual as a world-citizen instead of a nationalist, which cut down rapidly on wars. Scientific progress seemed to have gone on with only normal hitches, without any Dark Ages to set it back, and at a time when the people of Earth were sunk in their black-est pit of ignorance since the Stone Age, Llyrdis had atomic power, an established commerce with her neigh-bor planets, and was building and launching the first starship, which brought the history to its initial chapter, and Orthis.

"It is difficult for us now to realize what the first epic flight of man between the suns was like . . ."

Not as it was now, swift and easy, far outrunning the velocity of light. Science had the techniques even then to build and power the fast ships, but they were useless. Man could not survive the ultra-speeds. They had to go as they went between the planets, slowly. Four genera-tions lived and died within the close confines of that first feeble forerunner of the Vardda fleets, men and women dedicated in themselves and their children to the con-quest of the greatest barrier humanity had ever crossed and they crossed it. Slowly, painfully, exposed to all the dangers of unknown radiations and unexplored, un-charted wilderness in its most ultimate sense, exposed to the most terrible loneliness and isolation that living beings had ever endured, they toiled their way to a land-ing on the world of another star and then—and this, to Trehearne, seemed the most incredible bravery of all—they took off again for Llyrdis, which to this intermedi-ate generation was only a name and a tradition, and which they knew they would never live to see. Orthis was born during this return voyage, twenty-two years out from the planet he was taught to regard as home, though he had no knowledge of planets, nor of any life except that of the ship that moved apparently forever through the night of deep space. His ears must have been attuned only to that outer silence, his sight to the darkness and the far-off stars. To wind and rain, to sunlight and warm grass, to beasts and birds and the faces of many people, he was a stranger.

And a stranger he remained. "He could not endure to be planet-bound, after living all his life in space. He built his laboratory ship and worked in it, cruising where he wished and almost alone, for another fifteen years. Then, when he was thirty-seven, he announced his discovery—the birth of Galactic Man, the inception of the Vardda.

"Orthis refused to give to anyone the whole secret of his mutational process, believing that it was too dangerous in inexpert hands. He himself constructed the apparatus and used it, sowing with his own hands the seed of the Vardda race that would flower in the next generation. An at that time, he was revered by the people of Llyrdis almost as a demigod. But within the next year the troubles arose that almost split the Llyrdian State, and brought Orthis eventually into disgrace. He had given his discovery first to his own people, and now . . ."

Trehearne read with the most intense interest, trying to pry between the stiff factual lines for whatever force it was that made men like Edri fly in the face of their own best interests. Orthis had no intention of limiting the Vardda race to his own world. He would share his mutational process with the other planets of Aldebaran, and eventually with the star-worlds the original expedition had visited, and which were highly civilized. He wished them all to share in the great new future of star-travel—they and all races that might be discovered in the galaxy with sufficiently high culture-levels to be worthy of it. But when this became known to the embryo Starmen it started a most violent reaction. All sorts of objections were raised, ranging from the selfish but, to Trehearne, quite sensible argument that the Llyrdians had the best right to the mutation, having taken all the chances and done all the work, and therefore they should keep it, at least for a while, to the solemn threat of war on a galactic scale. "Remember," said the President of the Council, "how we helped the more backward worlds of our own solar system to achieve interplanetary flight, and how they repaid us. Remember the wars we have already fought! Let us take thought before we scatter this great power broadcast among the stars."

They took thought, and in spite of the impassioned arguments of Orthis and his followers they would not be hurried into a decision. The situation became so tense that Orthis' laboratory ship was sealed and impounded, and Orthis himself placed under virtual arrest. The battle in the Council Hall dragged on for years, and from the accounts it seemed to Trehearne that those fathers of the Vardda-to-be had not acted entirely from a selfish desire to hang on to a good thing. They were faced with a tremendous problem for which there was no precedent, nothing to go on but their own thoughts and feelings. Some of the Council members—the Llyrdian Congressmen—were obviously motivated by sheer hard-headed self-interest. But there were others who tried honestly to be just, and justice to their own people came first. They were afraid to share the mutation, and the control of it, with anyone. They were afraid to throw open all the unknown doors of space onto Aldebaran. The Orthists were defeated.

Then came the end, the dramatic fireworks. The Orthist party arranged an escape for their leader. They helped him get his ship away. They saw him off into the dark void beyond the sky, and they thought that after all he would be victorious. But by this time the new Vardda race had begun to flourish, and some of them were old enough, just barely, to fly. They went out after Orthis, believing intensely in their own right, as he believed in his. Orthis himself was undoubtedly able to endure ultra-speeds, for it was a long and bitter chase. The new young Vardda partially disabled his ship, but even so he managed to elude them. There was no ultra-wave radar or radio in those days, and after all, the old man had cut his teeth on the stars. They lost him, and that was the end, of Orthis and his ship—all except the message in the drifting life-skiff that was picked up more than a

72

century later. And Trehearne thought, "Whether he was right or not, Orthis was the hell and all of man!"

He could understand why Orthism had hung on stubbornly all these centuries. Certainly a more noble dream had never been dreamed. For himself, though, he was rather glad it was only a dream. He liked being a Vardda. He liked things the way they were. It had worked pretty well for everybody, and looking back, he could think of an awful lot of people he would have hated to see entrusted with the power to get at their neighbors on other stars. Orthis, that solitary, space-born man, had seen only the ideal, the abstraction. The Council had extrapolated a reality.

He did not discuss the question with anybody. That night in the pleasure-garden had impressed upon him the fact that the whole subject was unhealthy, and especially for him. The thought of Kerrel arose sometimes like a dark shadow in his mind, and linked with it was a gnawing anxiety about Edri, whom he had not seen before he left—not for any reasons of caution, which he would have been ashamed of, but because Edri had gone away somewhere and was not to be reached. He had sent Trehearne a brief message wishing him luck, and that was all.

About Shairn he thought as little as possible. He didn't want to know what she was doing. He preferred to remember the two weeks he had spent at the Silver Tower as ending against a blank wall.

He read on in the thundering saga of Vardda exploration, opening the starways. He studied his laws and codes. And he studied the ship. His bunkmates were more than willing to show off their knowledge to a greenhorn, particularly one older than themselves. Perri explained to him the inner workings of the purring metal giants that drove the ships—adaptations of the cosmotron for use as a generator, with centrifuges keyed to ultra-speeds that created the fifth-order rays. Rohan let him punch keys on the computers that did astral mathematics—he was not much interested in those—and Yann taught him how to read the radar screens that functioned not by slow electro-magnetic waves but by rays akin to those that powered the ship, moving far faster than light. He listened in Communications to

Vardda ships talking across the galaxy in thin ghostly converse by those same super-swift rays. The Skipper unbent briefly and allowed him—and this was like realizing an impossible dream—to hold the controls of the *Saarga* in his hands.

Yann did a good bit of tolerant jeering. "You're just starting out, and it's still fun. Wait till you're as old in the game as I am." He was twenty-eight. "I've made nine voyages into the cluster, and I'm tired of it. All I want is my own ship, wich I will let somebody else fly while I sit comfortably on Llyrdis and catch up on my wine and women."

"Have you any chance of getting one?" asked Trehearne.

"This trip will do it."

Rohan let out a loud laugh. "Hark at him! Don't let him kid you, Trehearne. We do well, but not that well."

Yann said seriously, "I mean it."

"Would you mind telling me how?"

"I saved my money," Yann told him virtuously. Then he grinned. "Besides, you're forgetting that I spent almost a year on the ground, filling in for some damned Vardda factor that died. I didn't waste my time." He turned to Trehearne. "Wait until we hit that system. I'll show you things you never saw before. Real barbarism. Good people, though. I got along with 'em fine."

"I guess," said Trehearne, "that there are all kinds of worlds in the cluster."

"Just wait," said Rohan sourly. "You'll have a bellyful before you're through. There are beautiful ones, and picturesque ones, and very quaint ones, all right, and some are even civilized. But there's a hell of a lot that are just plain godawful. You must have guessed that there's a reason for the high pay on this run."

The great cluster of Hercules grew from a patch of hazy brilliance lost in the blaze and crash and thunder of the universe, to a monstrous star-swarm, blinding even through a darkened port—a swirling hive of suns, white, red, yellow, peacock blue and vivid green, booming across the eternal void with the rush and roar of a cosmic avalanche toward some unknown destination, guided by the evil blinking eyes of the Cepheid variables. The *Saarga* plunged in at last among the edges of

74

the swarm, and Trehearne discovered at least one reason why Edri had warned him about the Hercules run.

"All the globular clusters are bad," Yann told him cheerfully. "Omega Centauri—there's another one to break a starman's heart. A strong ship, a strong captain, and no imagination—that's what it takes for a voyage like this."

Trehearne was introduced to gravity tides and for the first time in his life he knew what real fear was. The generators throbbed incessantly. The *Saarga* groaned and shrieked in all her iron bones, moving in erratic bursts of speed and sudden brakings, pitching and swerving as she felt her way in through shoals of suns, fighting the complex, ever-shifting gravitational fields. Trehearne got the feeling that he was trapped inside a giant football being battered back and forth between the stars.

Yann grinned. "It gets worse as you go farther in."

It did. Trehearne thought it was impossible for any ship to live in those mighty cross-currents of gravitation as the suns thickened like swarming bees. Forty times a day he was convinced that his end had come, and his only comfort was that the Hercules cluster was a more noble place to die in than any he had seen on Earth. He wore out his emotional potential until he had no more to give and merely suffered the noises and the violent pitchings as the *Saarga* rolled doggedly on her way. He had an idea that they must be deep into the heart of the cluster, and was somewhat daunted to learn, when the ship made her first landing, that they were still only on the fringe. He was too far gone to care much. All he wanted then was solid ground under his feet.

He emerged from the airlock into the light of a waning star, inexpressibly dim and sad, and looked out over a shadowy plain that glimmered even at midday with the distant glories of other suns, burning unconcerned. The plain was barren, scoured to the underlying rock by the winds that blew across it, dry and withering and cold. But there was a town there, very neat and gay with colors. It made Trehearne think of too-bright cosmetics on the face of a corpse. The *Saarga* discharged food and ores and many small luxuries, receiving payment in gems of royal purple mined out of the grey rock by little

men with sorrowful eyes. The place began to get on Trehearne's nerves. His duties kept him by the ship, checking bills of lading, but he watched the people who came
out from the town. They were healthy, well-fed, well-
dressed. But their bodies were stunted, and even the
children's faces held a sadness that seemed as much a
part of them as their skin, seeping into them from the
dying sunlight and the dying soil. He saw the way they
looked at the great ship and the men who flew in her,
and how they glanced then at the hot flaming suns that
were beyond their reach. They did not talk much. They
only stood and looked. But once a group of children
crept close to him and a small boy asked, in the *lingua
franca* of the trade worlds, "What is it like to fly the
stars?"

The *Saarga* did not stay there long, and Trehearne
was glad. "Christ!" he said to Yann. "Those poor kids
would break your heart. Couldn't they be moved or
something? They're just dying slowly with their world."

Yann shook his head. "It's been tried, but it doesn't
work. At planetary velocities, even a relatively short hop
between stars takes years, and most people just can't
take it psychologically. They crack up in all directions,
or else they sort of wither and die. Besides, I suppose
there's a sort of interstellar ecology. Old worlds die, and
new ones are born, and if you started upsetting the normal balance you'd have every livable planet overrun
with more population than it could support."

Thinking of the children, Trehearne said, "Ecology,
hell. They're human beings."

Young Perri shrugged. "We all take our chances.
You'll get used to it. Anybody know where we touch
next?"

"It's on the board," Yann said. "A lovely place. Trehearne will like it. There aren't any people there at all."

Trehearne's education into the rights, privileges, and
duties of a Vardda were only beginning. The *Saarga*
slowed again close to a cumulid variable of the most evil
aspect and picked up a planet that turned out to be a
worthy child of its parent. "Here's where we earn our
money," Yann said. "Radiation suits, Trehearne. Full
kit. Only the Old Man is exempt from this."

"What do we do?" Trehearne wanted to know.

"We pick fungus," Rohan told him not joyfully. "It makes a particularly fine antibiotic when it's been treated, but meanwhile don't get it on you. It's poisonous as hell. And be sure your oxygen lines are clear. The air is full of methane."

"He doesn't care," said Yann. "He's still full of the wonder of new worlds."

"Jeer away," Trehearne said equably. "I am."

XI

TREHEARNE TRAILED OUT WITH THE REST OF THEM, ALmost the whole ship's company, to gather the weird harvest. The radiation-suit he wore was not too heavy in weight—it couldn't be, for men who had to do hard work—a simple coverall of flexible metallic fabric, with a phone-equipped helmet and a separate knapsack oxygen-pack that could be quickly replaced when its oxygen was worked out.

The world he stood on was like something out of nightmare. Fungi higher than his head grew thickly, like a gruesome travesty of a forest, and in colors ranging from black to crimson and a yellow like spilled brains. The giant star—a sick, mad star, Trehearne thought, like all the short-period true variables—brooded in the poisonous sky, past the maximum peak of its brilliance now but still pouring out its febrile energies in a purplish glare. Trehearne grimaced, and shook his head. "This," he said, "is a planet only Weizsacker could love."

Perri's voice came over the helmet phone, curiously thin but so close at hand that Trehearne started. "Who's Weizsacker?"

"An Earthman with a theory. He advanced the idea that most stars have planets."

Rohan said incredulously, "You mean that anyone ever doubted it?"

"Oh, yes. Matter of fact, the general belief still is that Sol is unique in possessing planets, and that Sol Three, otherwise Earth, is unique in possessing life, particularly intelligent life."

Rohan swore, and then he laughed. "I never heard of such conceit. I thought you said Earthmen were civilized. Only savages have that wonderful conception of their own importance."

Armed with curved knives and big sacks of a thin plasticoid substance as flexible as cloth but air tight when it was sealed, the men spread out through the fungoid jungle. They kept more or less together in small groups. Trehearne could hear them talking, a confusion of voices over the helmet phone. He talked a lot himself, not about anything in particular, just talking for the sake of hearing something human. There was a strange and increasingly unpleasant feeling of isolation, locked up in his armor, breathing artificial air, unable to see much because of the helmet that restricted his field of vision. He moved with difficulty over spongy dust that sucked him down almost to the knees at every step. The light was lurid and hard on the eyes, and the ugly growths grew uglier by the minute, their vivid colors more revolting. It was hard to tell who was near him, with everyone masked out of human semblance by the shapeless suits. He tried to keep close to Yann and the two youngsters, checking them by voice.

"Don't bother with the big ones," Yann told him. "They aren't any good. Here, see the little pretties just coming up? Those are what we want."

Trehearne looked doubtfully at the size of his sack, and then at the nasty little mushroom-like heads thrusting up from the ground. "It'll take a long time to fill this thing."

"Hours. Might as well dig in."

Trehearne began patiently to work, bent over double or squattering clumsily along on his knees. The uncleanness of the place began to get on his nerves. Unavoidably he broke the adult growths from time to time and was showered with sooty black, or liverish pink, or ugly red and yellow dust, or was enveloped in clouds or

78

spores. He tried to watch the others, but he lost track of them now and then. Sometimes they did not answer when he called them. A slow claustrophobia grew on him and had to be fought down. He sweated heavily inside his armor. His muscles tired, and still the huge sack was not filled.

The light of the cumulid star began visibly to fade. Trehearne looked around. A wall of leprous color closed him in. There was no one in sight. "Yann?" he called. "Perri?"

"Hoi!" That was Perri. "Dull work, isn't it?"

"Disgusting. Where's Yann?"

"I don't know. Yann?"

"Here, damn it. If you'd pick more and talk less we'd be out of this pleasure garden sooner."

Trehearne could not place their positions. They sounded alike, all as though they spoke inside his own helmet. He worked on, hoping to catch sight of someone. The sick sun had worn out its burst of energy and was sinking into exhaustion, dimmer, redder, with the effect of an abnormal sunset. A kind of shadowy dusk crept between the feet of the tall distorted growths. Trehearne began to feel uneasy. He knew it was only the cumulative effect of the surroundings and the prisoning armor. He refused to pay attention to it. But it would not go away. It came in waves, with a prickling of nerve-ends and a lifting of the hair. He continued doggedly to throw the small fungi into his sack. He wanted to talk now more than ever, but he was afraid to, afraid that his unreasoning fear would show in his voice and disgrace him. He began to make long swings back and forth, trying to find somebody, but he could not, though he knew they must be close by. He was very hot, but his back turned cold and trickles of icy moisture ran down it. The unhealthy dusk grew thicker, and the shadows were red. He began to see movement out of the tail of his eye, as though something or someone walked stealthily just out of sight behind the screening growths.

"Yann?"

"What?" The bodiless, distanceless voice, speaking thinly in his ear.

"There's no life here, is there? I mean, outside of these stinking mushrooms."

"Not that anyone knows about. Why?"

"Nothing. It was only a trick of the shadows, I guess."

"Getting nervy, little Earthling?"

"Listen, the hell with you and your smart cracks."

"Think nothing of it," Yann said unabashed. "We all get nervy. I'm almost finished. How about you?"

"Pretty soon."

"Well, hurry up."

Silence. An occasional burst of voices over the helmet phones, confusing, jumbled. The men weren't talking so much now. They were tired, and the place oppressed them. Their spirits were going down like the light of the sun, sprawling hugely over half the sky with the red light running out of it like blood. Trehearne watched the shadows constantly, turning uneasily round and about with a blind feeling at his back. His nerves still pricked and rippled, and would not be quieted.

His sack was nearly full. He thought about the ship, about lights and familiar faces and getting off the suffocating armor. There was a monstrous fan-shaped growth glaring crimson in the sinking glow. It was flanked on one side by a bloated puffball colored black, and on the other by a crinkled, convoluted monster blotched with brown and yellow. It had at its feet a brood of little ones, enough to fill the remaining space in Trehearne's sack. He walked toward it, brushing by the blotched and convoluted thing. He felt at his back a sudden tug and a snapping. He turned, floundering in the soft mould with his heavy boots. He turned as fast as he could but there was no one, nothing, and then it dawned on him what had happened. His oxygen line had been ripped loose.

He began to shout. He didn't mind using his breath. He had very little left to use. He shouted in wild panic and began to run, nowhere in particular, butting and stumbling into the fungi, searching desperately for someone to help him before he died. "Where are you?" the voices were clamoring in his helmet. "Where are you?" And he kept screaming, "Here!" as though the word had any meaning, as though they could tell from the sound of his voice whether he was ten feet or half a mile away. The automatic valve-seal had closed at once to prevent the escape of what air there was in the armor, but it was getting hard to breathe. His lungs would exhaust the last of the oxygen in a minute or two, and then he could either suffocate in his armor, or rip off his helmet and burn his insides out with the methanated poison this world used for atmosphere. It was a lousy way to die and he didn't like it, and he couldn't figure out how it had happened. He must have fouled his line on some part of the fungus, that nasty one that looked like a monstrous brain. He must have passed too close to it and got hooked on some tough projection . . . It was getting dark and he was sick at his stomach and his lungs were pumping, laboring, achieving nothing.

He tried to yell again, and couldn't make it. His knees caved under him and he fell, almost into the arms of a shapeless but human figure that was saying a lot of things he couldn't understand. He felt himself rolled over. There was a moment when the darkness closed down almost completely and then a stream of oxygen, pure and fresh, poured into his helmet. The mechanism that had so nearly stopped began to work again, not smoothly, with a good deal of gagging and choking, but working. Somebody's voice penetrated to him, telling him for God's sake not to get sick in his helmet, and he managed to sit up and look around.

Two men were bending over him, and a third stood behind them. He could recognize them through their face-plates. None were his bunkmates. There was somebody else behind him, holding him up. Voices were still clattering inside his helmet, demanding to be answered. He thought he heard Rohan and Perri, but he wasn't sure. "Who's that behind me?" he asked. His own voice came out as though there were hooks on it. His throat hurt. "Who's there?"

"Me. Yann. Welcome back, Trehearne. I thought for a minute you'd gone over the edge."

"Damn near it." His tongue felt like a feather bolster. "I don't know what happened . . ."

"Your air-line got snagged," said one of the men helpfully, telling Trehearne no news. He grunted and said,

"But how? I thought I must have hooked it on one of these ugly brutes, but they break so easily . . ."

"They toughen up as they age. Look here." The man

81

reached out and took a horny protuberance in his hand. "Plenty of resistance, especially if your coupling was not properly tightened."

He didn't remember any such protuberances, and the blotched brain-shaped thing had looked bright and youthful. But he let it drop. He didn't know quite what other answer there could be, and right now he didn't want to think about it any more. Everything was lost in an overpowering desire to get back to the ship. He started to flounder up onto his feet, and Yann's powerful arm helped him. "Anyway," he said to the men in front of him, "thanks for saving my neck."

"Thank Yann. He had your air-line recoupled by the time we came. You were running right toward us, but you might not have made it if he hadn't found you first."

Trehearne turned round to face Yann. "Thanks."

"No trouble at all. I don't say I'd save you out from under the claws of something or other at the risk of my own skin, Trehearne, but since this was a simple task, think nothing of it. I was just lucky to find you. And next time don't stray so far away." He grinned and shoved Trehearne forward. "You aren't finished yet. You still have to explain to the Old Man why you lost your sack."

"Oh God," Trehearne muttered. But he didn't turn back. If the Skipper wanted that sack he could go and look for it. For the time being, Trehearne was through.

The *Saarga* creaked and groaned and lurched her way deeper and deeper into the cluster, touching like a tramp freighter at this port and that one, wherever there was trading to do and cargo to be had. Only her ports were planets, and her seas were the nighted gulfs between them. The memory of what had happened on the world of the variable star faded out of Trehearne's conscious mind, though he sometimes started awake in his bulk with the ghastly feeling of suffocation strong on him from a dream. But the succession of places and peoples, ever-shifting, ever-new, gave him too much to think about to waste his time brooding over something that was over and done. Insensibly, through habit and association, he was losing all sense of personal strangeness, becoming as thoroughly a Vardda as though he had been born on Llyrdis. Some of the first fine childlike glow of wonder wore off. It began to seem the most natural thing in life to go between the stars as between islands. The interest remained, but the feeling of awe departed.

They touched at systems that had a high degree of civilization, where Trehearne first saw the Vardda factories, vast walled compounds held under treaty, and crammed with warehouses full of goods from all over the galaxy. The system of the compound, the separate landing field, and the Vardda factor were universal wherever there was trade enough to warrant them, even on barbarian planets. "That's where the fortunes are made," Yann told him, and grinned. "I know. A few years in a factory, and you can retire."

Trehearne made a mental note of that, though he had no wish to be a factor. The *Saarga* moved on. They traded with scaly humanoids under the glare of a blue-white sun. They stripped the worlds of a red giant, leaving cheap gilded trinkets in exchange for rare radioactive minerals, and the small wide people felt themselves enriched. Trehearne had been amazed at the persistent recurrence of the humanoid form even when the root-stock from which a particular race had evolved was not even remotely human, and Yann had explained to him what every Vardda school-child was taught in General Biology, that the development of the humanoid form (i.e., possessing a recognizable head, carried in a vertical or erect posture, two lower limbs used for purposes of locomotion, and two upper limbs used for manual tasks) rested simply upon the necessity of a species that intended to progress beyond the animal level of intelligence to evolve hands, or a workable substitute, and free them for use.

But human or humanoid, furred, scaled, feathered, or normally integumented, of whatever color or size or state of social development, one thing was common to all the races of all the worlds. They hated the Vardda. It was a hatred based purely on envy, and Trehearne became so used to it that he hardly thought about it any more, except to notice its variation according to cultures —the aboriginals who mixed with it a worshipful, superstitious fear of the Vardda starlords, the barbarians who would have killed them except that they were greedy for the luxuries of trade, the civilized folk who treated them with cold respect and ate their hearts out with jealous longing. The only thing that really bothered Trehearne was the children, especially the young boys, who followed the Vardda up and down the streets and as near as they were allowed to the ship, asking over and over the same eternal question—"What is it like to fly among the stars?"

He had almost forgotten Earth. And then they swung in toward the world of a yellow sun, a green world that tore his heart quite suddenly with a rush of memories. He stared out the port at distant fields and trees, and at a city that might have been an Earthly city, shorn of its dirt and slums and spreading along the bank of a mighty river, and he was astonished that he could still feel homesick.

Yann looked at him sourly. He was brushing and sprucing up his uniform, and Rohan and Perri were brushing theirs, and none of them looked happy.

"Looks pretty, doesn't it?" said Yann.

Trehearne nodded. He was looking at the river and thinking of the Mississippi. His mind was a long way off.

"Well, it is pretty," Yann muttered. "The climate's fine, the people are civilized, the women are handsome, and I'll bet even the food is good. But we're not allowed to enjoy them. We aren't even—"

The buzzing signal of the ship's intercom interrupted him, and the captain's face appeared on the small telescreen.

"This is a warning, and a reminder. Here is where we do our trading with our hats in our hands and a humble look. Have you got that, all of you? You are to remain within the trading compound. You are not to fraternize with the natives. You are to show all deference to such members of the Hedarin as you may have contact with. And you are *not*, under any circumstances, to take offence at anything that may be said by them. In other words, keep your mouths shut until you're forced to open them, and then sing small. Those are orders, and I'll discipline any man that breaks them!"

The screen went dark. Trehearne looked at the others. "What kind of a place is this?"

"You heard the Old Man. It's a place where the Vardda apologize for living."

"Who are the Hedarin?"

"The lawgivers. The wise men. The speakers of the last word."

Young Perri gave his shoulders an expressive twist. "Creepy beggars," he said. "They're parapsychs."

XII

THE COMPOUND WAS LARGE AND CHIEFLY EMPTY, except for an open-sided building like a fair pavilion at one end of it. There was no factory, only the compound adjoining a landing field, outside the city. Large crowds were gathered beyond the low walls, much like any crowd on Earth, laughing, pushing, pointing at the ship, sending up an incessant gabble of talk. But the compound had only a few dozen men in it. They were inside the pavilion, waiting, and Trehearne was treated to the unusual spectacle of the Vardda captain and his officers marching humbly forward to ask permission to trade.

"Come a little closer," Yann whispered to him. "See those two tall men in the dun-colored robes, sitting at the back? They're Hedarin. Watch."

The Vardda officers spoke to the two men, and received a brief answer. "They give us two days," said Rohan. "Generous of them." Trehearne looked longingly over the compound wall. There were clumps of trees out there, and it must be coming on to fall, for the leaves were turning. The sky was intensely blue, with a soft haze low in the horizon, and the air was crisp. If you didn't look too closely it might be Ohio in October, and he wanted to go somewhere and walk alone, remembering. He didn't know why. Earth was behind him, and he did not regret it. But he wanted to go and walk among the turning trees.

Instead he got out lists and manifests and stood by, while the trading began. Goods and samples of goods, from trinkets to medicines and light machinery were brought out of the ship, and the bringing was done by the Vardda themselves. Trehearne helped, and all the cursing that was done was done quietly. "Too goddam proud to supply porters," somebody said. "The people wouldn't mind, but the Hedarin think it's debasing. Not the physical labor, you understand, but even the appearance of working for us. Me, I'd let 'em rot before I'd trade with them."

"The Old Man doesn't feel that way, so tail on, will you? This crate is heavy."

In the pavilion, the business went briskly. Only the Hedarin, sitting aloof, seemed unfriendly. Their faces gave Trehearne a peculiar feeling. Rather too small for their massive heads, though not so much as to be deformed, their features had a sort of iron strength that was almost chilling, as though the mind behind them had overswayed all the weaknesses of the flesh. Their eyes, deep set and light in color, seemed to look inward, not in the usual foggy contemplative way of people pondering over their thoughts, but as down a bright, clear vista where nothing was dark or doubtful, where no trivia could exist, no stirrings of emotion, no wayward impulse. They were splendid looking men. He had to admire them. But there was no thought of liking them. They watched the trading, and Trehearne began to notice that every item was offered for their approval before any bargain was struck. Most often it was granted, but now and then there would be a shake of the head and the article was rejected. The merchants might look regretful, but they did not protest.

"They swing an awful lot of weight," Trehearne said under his breath to Yann.

The First Officer, a slightly greying man who knew the Cluster like his own flower garden, was standing near and heard him. "So would you," he said, "if you could look inside a man's head and see all his thoughts, and into his body and trace the course of every gut, simply by using the power of your own mind."

"Uncomfortable people to have for rulers."

"They don't rule, in that sense. They're the physicians, the judges, the scientists—purely intellectual, a separate caste. They wouldn't stoop to anything as physical as ruling. They live entirely in and for the mind. In temporal matters they merely advise."

Remembering a certain Dr. Rhine, Trehearne asked, "Can they do everything? I mean, teleportation, telekinesis, telepathy, all the tricks?"

"They never discussed it with me, but I should think they could do all that, and more."

"Insolent bastards," said young Perri, scowling. His Vardda pride was hurt. Rohan kicked him. "Keep it to yourself. And don't even think too loud." Trehearne fidgeted. For the moment there was nothing to do, and he was standing with the others, six or seven of them, waiting. Finally he whispered, "What do we get here that makes it worth while?"

"Gem-stones," said Yann. "Fabulous. And their lapidaries rank as just about the best in the galaxy." He bent his head very close to Trehearne's and whispered, "All the same, I agree with Perri. Look at those merchants. Damned if I'd let anybody tell me what I could buy, and what I couldn't."

The Hedarin were out of earshot, and no whisper could possibly have carried to them over the buzz and chatter of the trading that was going on in front of them. Yet all at once they turned their heads, and Trehearne found himself looking straight into the glare of those clear eyes. He felt Yann start involuntarily, and then something passed like a cold wind through his mind, touching every hidden corner of it with a casual ease that horrified him, and dropping it immediately after with an unmistakable contempt that enraged him. He shook his head in a futile but instinctive attempt to clear it of the invading presence and started forward in a blind temper, forgetting orders completely. The First Officer grabbed him and whispered fiercely, "Shut up!", though he hadn't said anything yet. The cold something winked out of his mind like a light going off. Out of the corner of his eye he saw the disturbed, astonished faces of his comrades, and he knew that the same thing had happened to them. And then a sudden glance passed between the Hedarin. They rose. One held up his arm and said, "The trading is ended."

All sound ceased at once. The merchants stood, disappointed and surprised, looking at the Hedarin, and then out of the uncomfortable silence came the voice of the Vardda captain, held rigidly under control. "But you gave us two days!"

"It is ended. Take up what is yours, and go."

The captain's voice was not now as polite. "I wish to know why. We've kept all the conventions . . ."

"We gave permission. Now we revoke it."

They gestured to the merchants, busy middle-aged men who looked like all the businessmen Trehearne had ever seen. Reluctant, but obedient, they turned away and began to walk out of the pavilion. Somebody—it sounded like the captain—said, "Of all the goddamned high-handed . . ." And then some other Vardda voice shouted to the merchants, "What are you, a bunch of children to be ordered around? Why don't you trade if you want to?"

One of the merchants answered, "The Hedarin are wise."

"Maybe," said Trehearne angrily. "Or maybe they just like to show off." He demanded of the men in the dun-colored robes, "What have you got against us?"

They did not answer, and Rohan said, laughing, "The same thing all the non-Vardda have against us. Also, we're crass, crude traders. We don't think."

"You think," said the Hedarin quietly. "And we do not want your thoughts. Among you there is more than baseness. There is murder."

Again there was a silence, and this time it had a quality of shock. The Vardda looked at one another, and suddenly Trehearne's spine turned cold. Shadows under a waning star, an ugly forest tight around him like a leprous wall, a tug, a snap, and death, unseen and unexplained but very capable, closing on him like a great dark fist.

Murder?

Voices, Vardda voices, aroused, indignant, challenging. The merchants were leaving, and the Hedarin had stepped down. The Vardda were demanding proof.

It couldn't be. No one aboard the *Saarga* had anything against him. It must have been an accident. There was no reason to think it wasn't.

"Who is it?" roared the captain. "You can't make an accusation like that and then walk out . . ."

"We have no part in your affairs. You demanded a reason, and it was given. That is all."

Murder. It was an ugly word. Trehearne wished they hadn't said it. He wished the episode of the air-line hadn't happened. It opened the way for so much speculation. It made him apply the threat to himself, when after all, every member of the crew probably had at least one enemy he wouldn't mind killing. Everybody thought about it at one time or another. He had thought himself about killing Kerrel, but thinking was one thing, and doing it another.

Kerrel. Could he have hired somebody, to see that a certain Earthman did not come back from the Hercules cluster?

Say he did. Who? Rohan? Perri? Yann? No, Yann had saved his life, and he couldn't see either of the youngsters in the role of a killer. Somebody else, then. He looked around at the familiar faces, angry now, resentful. Who? He could not pick one out. He knew them all. They were his shipmates. They might do a lot of things, but—murder?

The First Officer said a scatological word. "You could probe into any man's subconscious mind and find a wish to kill. It doesn't take a parapsych to know that. They just wanted an excuse."

"Yeah," said Yann. "The hell with 'em. Well, let's pick up our traps and go."

Trehearne thought the First Officer was probably right. It was the most comforting explanation. He clung to it. It seemed that if anyone had really wanted to kill, and had tried once, he would have tried again. They'd been to a lot of worlds and done a lot of things. There had been plenty of other chances.

Or had there? Who knew what might appeal to a murderer as a good chance? And he couldn't just kill.

He had to make it look like an accident. That wouldn't be so easy.

Oh, hell, forget it. It *was* an accident.

He did forget it, deliberately, as much as he could. But a certain uneasiness stayed with him, and he dreamed more often of the fungoid forest and the ghastly sensation of breathing without air. He began to want a change. He wouldn't have believed it a few months before, but he was getting sick of the ship, the confinement, the close quarters, the manufactured air and the palatable but synthetic food. He was not the only one. The most hardened veterans aboard were suffering from the ennui of a long voyage. They looked forward more and more to the landings, even on unpleasant worlds, and grumbled because they were so brief. By the time the *Saarga* reached the system of the green star, the terminal point whence she would start the equally long return voyage, Trehearne was so hungry for land that even that lurking unease was thrust out of his mind by the sheer joy of making worldfall.

Yann was full of excitement. "This is the system I told you about, Trehearne—the one where I was factor so long. I got to know the natives like a brother." He laughed and clapped Trehearne on the shoulder. "We make a good stop here, and when our work's done I'll show you some things!"

The *Saarga* set down on a world of emerald heat. Besides the starship the landing-field contained half a dozen battered interplanetary craft, brought out piecemeal by the Vardda and operated by them between the wild planets of the system. The great stockaded factory was one of the largest Trehearne had seen and the strangest.

The "logs" that formed the stockade and made the walls of the warehouses were of crystal, cut from the crystalline forests that covered much of the land. Trehearne thought of them as trees and forests, simply because they had stems and branches, but they were inorganic, the glittering proliferation of sublimated alien chemicals. They glowed and flashed under the fierce green sun, showing glints of weird color where a prism formation broke the light. And also, in their shining branches, they netted the many-colored rays of the brighter stars that burned even in the daylight sky.

90

There was a town beyond the factory. It too was built of the crystal logs over foundations of black rock sunk in the ooze. Thick vines clambered everywhere, bearing bulbous fruit. Undergrowth, green almost to blackness, stood between the trees. There was a smell of fragrant rottenness, cloying, sweet.

Trehearne worked his long shifts, moving and sweating through a bath of molten jade. It was a large world and heavy. The gravity dragged at him. The letters of the freight lists swam under his eyes. When his own job was finally finished, he found Rohan and Perri still hard at it, but Yann was through and waiting for him.

"Come on with me now," said Yann, and smacked his lips. "Wine, cooled in deep wells. Make a new man of you."

"A hell of a world," said Trehearne.

"You should see the others of this system. This is the pick of the lot."

They walked through the outer compound, a sort of caravanserai crowded with folk from the other planets, brought in for the trading. Cold-blooded creatures with crimson eyes, ophidian princes of the inner worlds, wrapped in golden mantles against the chill. Slim, furred kings of the outer planets, capped and girdled with precious stones, still and panting in the heat. These and others watched the two tall Vardda, thinking their own thoughts.

They passed through the gate out of the factory, wading in soggy mud. The sun was setting in a welter of lurid green, tinged with peacock hues. Trehearne looked at the town ahead, the straggling lanes, the crystal huts that crouched in sordid beauty, the encircling forest of ungodly trees. Doubt assailed him.

"Perhaps we should stay in the factory. There'll be plenty of wine and more comfort."

Yann cursed him good-naturedly. "I told you I know these people better than I know my own children! Come on, Trehearne, there's nothing to do in the factory. Don't you want to see something new?"

Trehearne did. He was sick of the factory, after those long shifts of sweating labor. He shrugged, and made sure of the prismed shock-tube in his belt. It was customary, when the Vardda went abroad on strange

91

worlds, for them to carry a weapon. They were sometimes needed. Yann noticed the gesture and grinned. His own belt-holster was empty.

"I'd feel safer with one myself," he said, "but these people we're going to see are my friends. They'd be mortally offended if I came armed—a sign I didn't trust them, you see, and then look out!" He led the way down the muddy road, and Trehearne followed.

Night came. The glorious sky of the cluster crashed down on them, sown to bursting with stars as bright as moons. The crystalline trees took on opaline fires. The hut walls glittered. Around the two Vardda gathered a crowd of sloe-eyed children, silent and solemn, with hides of dusky green. Women watched them from the doorways. Human enough and pretty enough too, the younger ones, sleek and olive-colored, wearing bright silks from Llyrdis about their hips and baubles in their hair.

Yann chattered happily as they went along the winding lanes, telling of his multifarious sins and adventurings and the clever ways in which he had cheated the factory. The hostile curious eyes of the women followed them and now and again a man spat expressively into the mud behind them.

They came at last to a hut on the outskirts of the town. Beside it were chained four pairs of beasts the size of harriers, milk-white with dark muzzles and feet, the undulating bodies built light and long for speed. They made shrill barking sounds and leaped at the strangers, showing hungry fangs. Trehearne thought they looked like gigantic weasels—and quite as friendly.

"Hounds," said Yann. "Kurat is a hunter. I had a private arrangement with him for skins." He winked hugely and lifted up his voice, shouting in the native tongue an obvious demand for Kurat to come out and welcome his brother.

A lean, hard-muscled man emerged. He wore a loincloth of brilliant blue silk, not very clean, and a necklet of hammered metal. He greeted Yann with glad cries. Trehearne smiled inwardly. They were two of a kind, the Vardda and the hunter, a brace of happy scoundrels. Kurat welcomed him in the *lingua franca* of the factory towns. A brother of Yann, it seemed, was his brother also. He swept Trehearne before him into the hut.

There was a numerous family inside. A very old man and woman sat in a corner, doing nothing. Babes and children cluttered the floor. Kurat's hulking wife waded imperturbably among them. A handsome younger woman brought in a great sweating jug and poured from it into Trehearne's cup. The wine was cold and bitter. Trehearne, draining it, began to forget the heat and his weariness. Then, as he looked up into the young woman's face, he was startled by the hatred in her watching eyes.

He said suddenly, "Why do you hate us so?"

She laughed metallically. "Is there any world where the Vardda are loved?"

"Because we are able to fly the stars and you aren't?"

"Because we too could have had the stars and you Vardda kept us from it!"

Trehearne stared at her, disconcerted by her sudden passion. "But the secret was lost . . ."

"Oh, yes! And even on this far world we know how it was lost! All the universe has heard of Orthis and of how the Vardda drove him into the depths of space and destroyed him because he would have shared his knowledge. And so you are free and I am chained, and my children after me forever."

She turned abruptly away from him. He looked after her, depressed by their new proof of what bitter depths of hostility lay behind the faces of the non-Vardda.

But Yann shook his shoulder. "Kurat has made a kill today—a rare skin. Come outside and look at it. It could be worth a lot of money."

Less from interest than to escape his own oppression, Trehearne rose. They went out a back way. There was a shed some distance away, where Kurat said the hide was drying. Yann and he chatted in the unfamiliar jargon. Trehearne was not much interested in the whole business.

It was dark inside the shed. Yann said, "Wait a minute while I make a light."

Trehearne waited but not long. The light exploded inside his own skull. He heard Kurat grunt behind him with the exertion of the blow, then laugh. Yann was laughing too.

Trehearne knew a moment of murderous fury and then the world of the green star slipped away from under him.

When it returned again into his ken, he was sprawled on his face in mud, stripped of his tunic, his jewelled belt, his shocker and his sandals. The hut of Kurat had vanished, the town with it. He was in the forest, encircled by trees whose crystal branches glittered under the savage stars. His head hurt violently.

He got unsteadily to his feet with only one thought in his mind—the determination to get his hands on his good friend Yann. He took three steps in no particular direction—and then stopped, bathed in a sudden icy sweat.

In the distance and not too far away he heard the high-pitched cry of Kurat's strange hounds.

XIII

TREHEARNE'S MIND CLEARED WITH AN ALMOST PHYSI-cal wrench. The fumes of the wine left it, and the thick obscurity put there by the blow. The pain stayed, but he could think. He could remember. The world of the cumulid star. The man in the dun-colored robe saying, Murder.

Murder. Yann.

Don't thank me, it was Yann that saved you. He had your air-line recoupled . . .

Crazy. It couldn't be Yann.

It was. He had followed him meekly into a trap and sat there meekly drinking while Yann and Kurat talked jovially over his head, arranging the details.

The cry of the pack was nearer.

They would not want his body in the hut or in the town. They would not want it to seem like murder. They would carry him into the forest, and then set the hounds after him, leaving the beasts to do the final work. Who could be blamed if a drunken Vardda wandered off where he had no business to be and was pulled down by a pack of hounds? He wondered if Yann and Kurat were following the hunt. He wondered why Yann wanted him dead.

Yann. The dirty treacherous son of a bitch . . .

Trehearne began to run.

The ropy vines that crept and clambered among the crystal trees were like nooses set to catch his feet. He fell, and rose, and ran again, and the spongy ground gave softly under his feet like sand. It was very hot, and he was heavy, heavy with the drag of a heavy world.

Behind him, clear and shrill, came the *yap-yap-yaahhh!* of Kurat's weasel hounds, racing over a fresh scent. The crystal branches gleamed and sparkled, tipped with star-fire, sharp-tipped like spears. Trehearne stopped and tried to break one and it was like trying to break a bar of steel with his bare hands. He gave it up and fled onward, not knowing where he was or where he was going, only wanting to stay away as long as he could from the lithe white demons that were hunting him. There was a little river, black and warm. He waded upstream in it, splashing to his waist, swimming in the deeper pools. The bitter wine had left him thirsty, and he drank. The water tasted foully of pitch and slime and he spat it out again, gasping. He heard the voice of the pack change to a querulous whining as they checked by the bank of the stream where he had entered it. He sank down to rest and listened to them casting back and forth. He thought he heard a man's voice shouting but he could not be sure. He went on again, striking away from the river and into the forest. The great stars were pounding against his head and his body was leaden with many extra pounds of weight by gravitation.

He prayed for a fallen branch, but there was none. He prayed to find the town and that too was denied him. He ran heavily under the glittering trees and behind him the hounds burst suddenly into full cry, more distant now but as chilling to the blood. It would not be long before they overtook him.

He measured the trees with an eye to climbing one for refuge. They were glassy and badly shaped, and they were low. He remembered the long whipcord bodies of the weasel-like beasts. He thought they could leap as high as they needed to pull him down. He staggered on, and every time he fell it was harder to get up again. A terrible rage was on him, rage against Yann. It wasn't fair. It wasn't fair to make a man run for his life on a world where he couldn't run. The cry of the pack came closer.

Abruptly, from somewhere ahead of him, rose the challenging voices of other hounds.

Trehearne stopped. He was caught now, between two fires. There was no use in going on. He choked on the acrid gorge of fear that filled his throat and cast about for a weapon, something, anything, to hold in his hands, to kill with, at least a little before he was torn apart.

It came to him that the yelping of the beasts ahead was stationary. It was irritable. They were not hunting. They were chained. Trehearne sobbed. He began to run again.

There was a clearing. He saw it ahead dimly through the starshine and the trees. He strove to reach it, and the pack-cry clamored at his heels. He tripped and pitched headlong and was almost happy, because he had fallen over a tangle of branches left from the breaking and clearing of the crystal trees. He caught one up. It was not long but it was sharp and heavy. It was better than nothing. He plunged forward with it into the edge of the open space, and there the hounds of Kurat bayed him.

Swift and undulant, white as frost in the starlight, they came leaping beautifully between the glistening trees. They cried out once, all together, and then they were still, still as arrows in mid-flight, arching toward him through the air. He set his back against a glassy trunk and swung his broken crystal branch. He struck some of them. But there were fangs set like hot irons in his flesh.

There was a hut in the center of the clearing. Four of the hunting-beasts were leashed beside it. They were the ones that had answered Kurat's pack. Now they snarled and screamed and fought their leashes. A man, a woman, and a tall boy came out of the hut. The boy started to run toward Trehearne, shouting. The man caught him. He spoke to the boy and made him be still. They stood there, watching.

Trehearne killed one of the hounds with his crystal club, and one he crippled. The remaining six boiled around him, a liquid tangle of bodies leaping, flowing, slashing with the white knives of their teeth. The blood ran on Trehearne's body. He swung and swung again, and yelled for help to the man and woman who watched stolidly.

They did not move. The boy tried to, and the man cuffed him.

Trehearne uttered a hoarse sound and dropped the branch. One of the brutes had fastened on his wrist. Its weight dragged him to his knees and he knew that this was the finish, the last of his voyaging amidst the stars. He tore the strong jaws out of his flesh and swung the brute as a flail in the faces of its mates and then he could hold it no longer and the pack closed in.

The boy had slunk back into the shadows by the hut wall. Now, suddenly, he reached and slipped the thongs from the necks of the tethered hounds.

They tore across the clearing over the jagged stumps and flung themselves upon the pack of Kurat.

For a moment the beasts forgot Trehearne. He scrambled free of the snarling tangle and went toward the hut. The man rushed by him, howling. He picked up a branch and began to beat the battling hounds, struggling to separate them. The woman wailed and ran to help him. The boy came to Trehearne.

He was not much above sixteen, tall and well made. He put his arm around Trehearne's waist and took him into the hut and sat him down. Trehearne was glad to sit. The room reeled and darkened around him. When his sight cleared the boy had brought cloths and a pungent salve and was binding his cuts.

"What is your name?" asked Trehearne in the *lingua franca*.

"Torin."

"You saved my life, Torin. I will not forget it."

"I would do anything for the Vardda." Instead of

97

hate there was hero-worship in this non-Vardda face. It was obvious that in the boy's eyes Trehearne was a figure of glory. Trehearne was touched.

Torin stared at him, his task forgotten. And he asked the question, the old unchanging question that was always on the lips of boys. "What is it like—what is it really like, to fly between the stars?"

Trehearne put his hand on the lean young shoulder and lied. "It is long and hard and not nearly as adventurous as hunting. I'll wager that you're as good a hunter as your father."

"Not yet," said Torin. "Some day . . ." He bent to his work again. His fingers moved over Trehearne's flesh, touching the muscles, spreading the wounds, gentle with the thick salve. He scowled, brooding over some question of his own. "It feels like mine," he said. "It bleeds like mine and here is an old scar and there will be new ones. It is not a different flesh, made of iron or some other thing."

He sprang up. "Look!" he cried. "I am strong, very strong. See, my flesh is hard like yours. Surely it is not true that only the Vardda can fly in the great ships! Surely I am strong enough to go out and see the stars!"

Trehearne could not meet his eager eyes. He said, "It takes a different kind of strength." He tried to explain and gave it up. He could only say, "I'm sorry."

He got up. "Will you guide me to the compound, Torin? And think what you would like out of all the things that are there. I can't take my life from you without giving something back—a little gift between friends."

Torin whispered, "I want to see the ship."

Trehearne frowned and in the interval of silence he heard the noises from the clearing—the whining growl of hounds and the sudden lifting of human voices.

"Your parents?"

"No," said Torin. "They are still trying to catch our beasts in the forest."

"Look out and see who has come, Torin."

He flattened himself in the corner behind the door. The boy opened it and peered.

"Two men," he whispered. "A hunter whose name is Kurat—and a Vardda." He drew back and looked at Trehearne. "They were hunting you?"

Trehearne nodded. His face had tightened and grown cruel. "Give me a knife."

Torin handed him a skinning blade of crystal chipped to a razor edge. Trehearne said, "Go and tell them I am dead from the hounds' tearing. Tell the Vardda to come and help you carry out my body."

Torin hesitated, then he went. Trehearne heard him calling across the clearing. The gabble of voices increased and Yann's familiar laughter sounded. The boy was talking, telling the details of Trehearne's dying.

Yann strode into the hut.

He came confidently. He had nothing to fear. And then Trehearne's arm was around his throat and the point of the knife was biting in under the angle of the jaw.

"Don't move," said Trehearne. And again, "Don't move!"

Yann stood still. Blood was running down the side of his neck. "You'll cut the vein," he whispered. "No deeper, please, no deeper."

He had not picked up any weapons on the way. There was none in his belt, none in his hands. Trehearne took the point of the knife out of Yann's throat and then he hit him. Yann fell sprawling on the floor. He started to complain, and Trehearne kicked him, as hard as he could with his bare foot, twice in the ribs, wanting to hear bone break. Yann's breath came out with a rush. Over his shoulder Trehearne said to Torin, wide-eyed in the doorway, "Keep watch, and tell me if anyone comes."

"They are busy with the hounds and with talking," the boy said. And then, "Will you kill him?"

"I'd enjoy it." Trehearne touched Yann again with his foot. "You tried it that other time, too, didn't you? God damn it, answer me! Didn't you?"

Coughing, his face against the floor, Yann muttered, "Yes."

"You crept up behind me, between those growths. You pulled my air-line loose and ducked before I could turn around. You went to a lot of trouble. Why did you save my life?"

Yann groaned and retched. "I'm sick."

"You'll be sicker." Trehearne got him by the hair of

the head, standing carefully and watching for any sudden move, and dragged him half erect. "Sit up and talk like a man. Why did you undo all your good work? You could have let me die right there."

Yann shook his head. "You were blundering straight into the others. Somebody was going to save you, and I figured it might as well be me. If you had any suspicions you'd switch them to someone else. Make it easier next time." His mouth twisted into a parody of a grin. "It did."

Trehearne said, "You're a hell of a nice guy." His hand moved and light flickered on the crystal knife. Yann's eyes were drawn to it.

"This wasn't my idea," he said. "I was only doing a job. You don't have to kill me." He put an emphasis on the pronoun.

"I don't have to. It's whether I want to or not. Whose idea was it, Yann?"

"He was going to give me a ship," Yann muttered. "A ship of my own. Any man would do it for a price like that. You'd do it yourself, Trehearne. That's just common sense."

Trehearne said, "Who offered you the ship?"

"Kerrel. You go fight it out with him. I've got nothing against you, Trehearne. Kerrel explained to me that it wasn't murder to put you out of the way, but a service to the whole Vardda community, and this was the only way he could do it. But I'm not interested in politics. This was just a business deal for me. One life, one ship."

"Kerrel isn't rich. Where was he going to get hold of a ship to give away?"

"I guess he had a deal in mind. Maybe that depended, too, on your not coming back. I don't know. Anyway, I can prove it was Kerrel. Here, I've got the whole business in writing. I'm no fool. Agent of the Council or not, a man's a man . . ." Still talking, still scowling, Yann dug into his tunic pocket. An instant later, an instant too late, Trehearne realized that by no possibility would Kerrel ever put such things in writing. He moved, fast.

The shocker came out of Yann's pocket, the weapon he wouldn't carry openly because Kurat would be offended, the weapon he had not left behind in the compound. Trehearne hit him just before the business end, the prism, cleared the silk cloth of Yann's tunic. He hit him with both hands, and he hadn't exactly forgotten the hunting knife with the razor edge, but he didn't care now, he didn't want to be laid out stunned and senseless by the shock-beam so that Yann could have his ship and Kerrel could have Shairn and the hounds could have their bellies full of meat. He hit him hard and rolled him over and rolled over with him. The shocker went skittering away, hitting the wall with a sharp click. Trehearne scrambled frantically to get to his feet first, but he didn't need to hurry. Yann was not going to get up any more. The shining haft of the knife was standing out of Yann's chest. It rose and fell a couple of times, and then it stopped. There was not much blood around it.

Torin broke the silence. "Will you kill the other one, too?" He jerked his head toward the door. Beyond it in the clearing Kurat was bawling at his yapping hounds.

Trehearne thought. He thought rapidly and clearly, and that was odd because there was a sickness in his belly, and a kind of shaking on him. After a moment he said, "No. There's a better way."

He went and picked up the shocker that had belonged to Yann. He then leaned over and took the slack of Yann's collar in his free hand and dragged him outside. He was very heavy, and his head lolled back against Trehearne's wrist.

Kurat turned and came toward the hut. There was a happy look on his face. He was a happy man. He had done a good job, for good pay. And then he saw Trehearne, and the shocker, and Yann lying on the ground where Trehearne had dropped him. Something queer and ludicrous happened to the face of Kurat.

Trehearne pointed. "There's a native hunter's knife in his heart. You killed him, Kurat. I saw you do it."

Kurat made a sound like something that has stepped into a snare and feels it closing. "I didn't. You lie, you know I . . ."

"You killed a Vardda," Trehearne said. "You were quarrelling over the wine, and you put the knife into him, so. That was wrong of you, Kurat. I don't think the

101

other Vardda will like it. I would go away, if I were you. I would take my hounds and my family and go a long way off into the forest."

Kurat stared for a moment into Trehearne's eyes. Then he looked at Yann. Then he turned and shouted up his bleeding hounds, saying no word but shouting with a curious raw edge to his voice, and went with them into the forest, running.

He was, Trehearne thought, no fool. He knew what Vardda vengeance could be, and he knew what his word would be worth against a Vardda. He did not think the factory would see Kurat again for many years. And he was glad. Kurat's disappearance would save Trehearne many explanations. He did not want to tell anyone now the truth of how and why Yann had died.

He did not want to talk about it except to one man.

XIV

TORIN'S PARENTS CAME BACK INTO THE CLEARING A few minutes later. The woman had three hounds leashed, all of them bleeding and one going on three legs. In his hand, by its loose scruff, the man carried the fourth one, dead. He flung it down at Torin's feet.

"There's your work," he said. "Two of the others will not hunt for days. We will go hungry because my son is a fool."

Then he saw Yann's body, and started back, looking swiftly at Trehearne.

"Kurat killed him," said Trehearne. "I'll take his body back to the ship. There will not be any trouble."

"I will help you," Torin said.

The man said nothing. He stood running his hard hands nervously up and down on his bare belly, a man oppressed by fate. The woman turned silently away to tie the hounds again. Trehearne took off his belt and pried two of the jewel stones out of it. They were not of the best, but to these people they were riches. He would have given them Yann's belt, which was more valuable, but he was afraid it would make them trouble when they tried to barter it. He put the two stones in the man's palm.

"Those will pay for your hounds. I'll leave word with the factor that they were not stolen. Just don't do anything till after the ship is gone." He lifted up Yann's body and laid it over his shoulder. "Come on, my friend Torin. Let's go."

He walked out across the clearing, and Torin came with him, pointing out the path. When they were out of hearing, he said to Trehearne, "I would like it if you could forgive my parents. To me they are good and kind, but they do not understand the Vardda."

"Perhaps they do," Trehearne said. "Better than you know."

It was morning when they reached the compound, a green morning oppressed with heat. Trehearne was ready to drop, and even the boy was weary. Yann had been a heavy burden, shared between them. But all the way he had talked of the great ship. He would accept no other gift but that, to see the ship, and he pleaded so that Trehearne had not the heart to refuse him. After all, it was little enough reward for what the boy had done.

"You will have to wait, though, perhaps a long while. I will have to do much talking, about *him*."

"I will wait," said Torin, smiling. "I have waited all my life."

It was the last great day of the trading and all the Vardda were inside the compound except one man who guarded the *Saarga*. The hatches were closed. Only the airlock port was open and the guard sat in front of it, yawning in the heat. He quit yawning when he saw Yann's body.

Things were a little confused for Trehearne for a while. He talked, and then he patiently endured the tongue-lashing the Skipper gave him. It was a rough one, such as a man deserved who would go drinking with a comrade and pass out and let his comrade be killed by natives. But when it was over there was nothing to do but order Yann buried and go on with the last trading. Trehearne was glad that Rohan and Perri were too busy right now to ask questions. When it was all finished he found Torin and went with him to the airlock port and spoke to the guard.

"He helped me out there. Maybe he saved my life. I promised him a look around."

The guard looked doubtful. "It's against the rules. The Old Man would have my head if he found out."

"How can he find out? He's busy. Don't worry, I'll see the boy gets clear of the ship. You can look the other way."

The guard could not withstand Torin's hungry gaze. He was a family man, with sons of his own. "Well—all right. Only be sure you get the kid out again—fast!"

Trehearne saw to it. He showed Torin what he could, from the bridge to the generator rooms, and the boy trod softly as though he were in a holy place, touching, sighing, wondering. Trehearne was sorry he had brought him. It was pitiful to see all that longing that could never be fulfilled. He pressed upon Torin what few trinkets from other star-worlds he had in his own possession and then led him out from the ship and stood with the guard, watching the boy go slowly away across the field, looking back, always back, until he was lost behind the compound wall.

"Poor little beggar," said the guard. "Star-crazy, like all the rest of them. Well, he'll get over it."

"I suppose so," said Trehearne, and was glad that he would not see Torin again.

He found the doctor and had himself patched up, and after that he was busy checking lading. He was dead for sleep, and it seemed an eternity until, toward midnight, the cargo was all aboard and the hatches locked. The *Saarga* lifted into the star-shot sky, and the acceleration built and built to the thrust of the humming generators.

Trehearne told Rohan and Perri that he was too played out to talk about what had happened, and tumbled into his bunk. He was almost instantly alseep—and almost as instantly awake again.

There was a screaming in the ship . . .

They found Torin lying beside the well that led up from the hold. He had made it that far. His skin was already darkened with the subcutaneous hemorrhage, his body twisted and writhing, his face almost unrecognizable. And he screamed and would not stop.

Trehearne held him and watched him die.

It seemed to take a long, long time. It was not a clean death. It was dissolution. Trehearne remembered his own torment and there was nothing he could do. The others watched also with sick white faces. In the end it was the guard who went to fetch a cloth to wrap the body in, and there were tears on his cheeks.

Trehearne laid Torin on the sheet. His flesh was not hard any more. He was no longer straight and well made. He was not even a dead boy. He was a rag, a shapelessness, an obscenity. It crossed Trehearne's mind how nearly he had come to dying that same death.

He got up. He returned to his cabin, stripped and scrubbed himself in a kind of frenzy. He kicked his sodden garments into the corridor for someone else to deal with. He could not touch them again. And all the time he heard Torin's voice crying, "Surely I am strong enough to go out and see the stars!"

They came a little later and told Trehearne that they had found where Torin had hidden himself under the wrappings of a bale, to be carried aboard with the cargo.

"It wasn't your fault," they told him. "There was no way you could have seen the boy."

Trehearne was not comforted.

They buried Torin in deep space, to drift forever among the suns of Hercules. And Trehearne thought of a hut, of a man and a woman who were waiting for their son to come home. He wished that Torin had listened the wisdom of his father.

The *Saarga* tramped her way onward among the worlds of the cluster. Time and events gave Trehearne other things to think about. He was a starman now, tested and hardened, a functioning part of his environment. His horizons were boundless and the stars had not lost their lustre. But somehow, even so, the first fine flush of glory was gone.

He remembered the bitterness of the woman who had said, "You are free and I am chained and my children after me forever." He remembered the countless young men who hungered, the eyes of children wide with dreams. Each time he saw the new-healed scars on his body he remembered the boy who had dressed those wounds and found the Vardda flesh no different from his own—a treachery too subtle for his understanding.

Over and over, when he slept, he held Torin in his arms and watched him die.

He told himself that it was all wasted pity. Whatever had been done to Orthis long ago was not his doing. Things were as they were and there was no help for it. He was one of the lucky ones and he should be content with that. Most of the time he was content. But now and again there would come the small sharp doubts, the creeping sense of guilt.

If only Torin had not come aboard the ship to die!

He needed to talk to Edri. He needed to ease his mind, to get things straight with himself, and he knew that Edri would understand.

He was glad when they started the long haul back to Llyrdis. He discovered that much as he wanted to see Edri, he wanted even more to see Shairn. He wondered if she had forgotten him by now or if she would be waiting when he landed.

The *Saarga* made her worldfall at last under the tawny-red glare of Aldebaran. Trehearne watched the golden planet rush and grow toward the ship. He cheered with the others at the first sight of home and did not think it odd that he should strain as eagerly as they to see the familiar towers of the city rising out of the mountain-girdled plain.

When the freighter found her dock and wallowed into it, Joris was on hand to watch his ship come in. He had been in contact with the *Saarga* by ultra-wave radio and now he boarded her before the ports were fairly open. The Skipper had given him good news of the venture and he was in jovial spirits, clapping shoulders all around, peering at manifests, firing questions, demanding to know how Trehearne had acquitted himself.

"A good voyage, eh?" he cried. "Too bad about Yann, but any voyage through the cluster is a good one if only one gets killed!"

Trehearne said bitterly, "Someone else did."

Joris stared at him, uncomprehending.

"Oh, not one of the crew. A native boy, crazy to fly the stars. He stowed away."

All the light went out of Joris' face, leaving it bleak. It was a long time before he spoke and then it was only to make a routine statement about the ship. He seemed to have lost all his joy in it. Trehearne was surprised at the impact that those few words about a nameless boy had had on the old man.

Joris left soon after. He told Trehearne, "I'll see you in a day or so. Meanwhile I think Shairn is waiting for you at the sector gate." He spoke as though his mind were not really on what he was saying. He turned away, then hesitated, and asked, "How old was that boy, Trehearne?"

"About sixteen."

Joris nodded. He walked away across the apron as though he carried on his massive shoulders some heavy burden that weighed them down. Trehearne signed over his manifests to the port official in charge of unloading and went in search of Shairn.

She stood outside the great barred gate, watching for him. She was just as beautiful as he remembered.

He said, "You haven't forgotten me then?"

"No. Did you expect me to?"

"I wouldn't have been surprised."

She laughed—the sweet familiar laughter spiced with mockery. "You're a wise man." She cocked her head back and studied him. "You've changed. You've got so brown and hard and—older. I think I like you even better now. But I'll have to learn to know you all over again." She pulled him toward the long, sleek vehicle that waited. "It will be nice," she said, "this getting acquainted again!"

The broad road took them northward along the coast,

away from the clamoring spaceport and the city. The cliffs rose from the golden sea, wild and forbidding.

She asked suddenly, "Where did you get that?"

His sleeve had fallen back and she was looking at the scars on his wrist.

"Someone set the hounds on me," Trehearne answered indifferently. Then, "By the way, how is Kerrel?"

"I haven't seen him." She glanced at the scars again. "How did he work it?"

"How did who work what?"

"Oh, stop trying to be subtle! I had a feeling that Kerrel might arrange something for that voyage. He's not a man who takes his defeats lightly."

Trehearne told her briefly the story of Yann and the hounds. He finished, "I want to see Kerrel."

"You will!" Shairn's eyes sparkled. "And I want to be there when you do!"

The car swung around a curve and there on its great crag loomed the Silver Tower—Shairn's ancestral home, built by generations of Varrda men and women who had reached out with strong hands to grasp the stars.

For a time, with Shairn, he forgot about Kerrel and Torin and all the things that preyed upon his mind. He only knew that it was very good to be here. It was evening when he was again reminded of them. They were sitting in the gallery, sipping the sharp, cold wines, and Shairn said, "Are you happy, Michael?"

He remembered another time when she had asked that question—the night that Edri had walked away alone down the avenue of trees. He remembered Edri crying out in the dark against injustice, and instantly the old restlessness was back upon him.

"Yes," he said. "Yes, I'm happy." He turned the wine-glass in his hands, brooding. "Shairn, could you get Edri out here? I'd like to see him."

He felt her stiffen and draw away and he thought that she was angry with him. He went on, "I didn't mean now. Tomorrow's time enough. But I—well, I want to talk to him."

"You're fond of Edri, aren't you?"

"He was a good friend to me."

"Yes—and to me." She was silent for a moment and

108

then she turned around. "You might as well know now as later. Edri was arrested a month ago."

Trehearne sprang up. "Arrested?"

"Yes. They sentenced him yesterday. Exile to Thuvis —for the rest of his natural life."

XV

FOR A MOMENT TREHEARNE STOOD STILL LIKE A MAN stunned. *Thuvis—for the rest of his natural life!*

He remembered that dark, inexpressibly lonely world of a dying sun that Shairn had shown him in the microfilm viewer, on the way from Earth.

"No," he said. "Not Edri. There must be some mistake."

Shairn shook her head. "I wish there were but there isn't. Edri is an Orthist, caught, confessed and convicted. He was unable even to offer a defense."

She turned away from him. "I don't like it either. But Edri knew what he was doing. He brought this on himself."

Trehearne asked, "What happened?"

"You remember that night in the wine garden when Kerrel spoke of a man named Arrin who had been arrested?"

"Yes. He was a friend of Edri's."

"Well, they couldn't find Arrin's papers. They wanted them very badly. It seemed that Arrin had found some clue to the course of Orthis' ship, on that last voyage when it was lost, and had been making calculations."

She paused, then added grimly, "Kerrel got the idea that Edri had those papers."

Trehearne's yellow eyes took on a peculiarly evil glint. "Then Kerrel was at the bottom of this?"

"Yes. It was his duty as agent of the Council to investigate, and he did, and very cleverly. Well, Edri had the papers all right, and more of his own."

Trehearne groaned. "The idealistic fool! Why wasn't he satisfied to be a Vardda himself, without worrying about the rest of the galaxy!"

Shairn seemed relieved. Then, "That's what *I* said! But knowing your friendship for Edri, I was afraid you'd lose your head when you heard."

She went on quickly. "I know you'll have a reckoning with Kerrel over this and your own score. But you'll have to be careful since he's a Council agent. I can help you—"

But Shairn's voice faded out of Trehearne's hearing except for that one phrase.

"—*knowing your friendship for Edri*—"

Yes, Edri had been his friend. He was sorry for Edri. But should he let friendship be a chain to drag him back down from all that he had dreamed and desired and finally achieved?

No! He would not let himself be trapped by friendship and by pity! He had been merely indulging in emotionalism, to sympathize as he had with the non-Vardda peoples' hunger for star-freedom, to remember as he had the hopeless longing in their eyes, to brood as he had over the dying of Torin.

A sick fatal foreboding grew in Trehearne as he realized the decision shaping in his mind. He knew that it was shaped by emotion, not by reason, and he felt a savage contempt for his own weakness.

He spoke, interrupting Shairn. "I'm sorry, Shairn, I was thinking. And I think I've got to try to help Edri."

She stopped, looking at him with wide steady eyes. Then, rapidly, "Michael! Don't be a fool!"

He smiled mirthlessly. "You've told me that before. I'm telling myself now. But it doesn't work. It seems that I'm determined to be a fool."

"You're taking it too tragically! After all, Edri's not going to be executed."

Remembering Edri's words about the fate of Arrin, Trehearne answered, "I think he'd almost prefer that.

110

Exiled to a remote star, never to fly again, nothing to do but sit and wait for death—"

"But there's nothing you can do, Michael! He's convicted, sentenced. They're taking him off tonight. So there's an end to it."

Trehearne rose to his feet. "I'm going back to the city, Shairn."

"For what?"

"I'm going to see if I can get him away."

She understood then the full depth and danger of his thinking. She caught him fiercely by the arm.

"Are you going to throw away everything you've worked so hard to get for nothing? Remember, Edri's a traitor. No matter how good a friend he was to both of us he's a traitor and deserves his punishment."

"That's how you feel, is it?"

"Is there any other way I could feel? You know what the Orthists are as well as I do."

He said quietly, "I'm not sure I do. Perhaps you'd better tell me."

"They're destroyers. They want to ruin Llyrdis, the Vardda empire, everything as it is now." Her passionate voice took in the star-trails, the swift ships flying, the Vardda pride of race and achievement.

"Orthis had his laboratory in his ship. The secret of the Vardda mutation is there. They want to find that ship. They want to find the secret in it and spread it all across the galaxy."

"Would it be so terrible," asked Trehearne, "if others should have the ability to fly the stars?"

She looked at him as though he had spoken blasphemy. He added, "Except, of course, that it would wreck the Vardda monopoly."

"That sounds very strange, coming from you," she said bitterly. "You, the outsider, who fought so hard to be a part of the monopoly. It looked pretty good to you then after thirty-three years of crawling in the mud of Earth!"

"I've seen more of it now. I've seen a boy die because of it. I don't think I like it any longer."

"You don't like it?" Her voice was low and passionate. *"You?* And what do you know about it? *We* earned the right to what we have. We were the first—first of all

111

the races of the galaxy to go into interstellar space. And we did it without mutation, without anything! Four generations that first voyage took. Four generations of children born in deep space, in a little ship crawling between the stars! No one else ever did that. No one else ever dared! And as for our wicked monopoly—it keeps the peace of the galaxy. It keeps worlds alive that would have died. It brings wealth and comfort where they never were before. But *you* don't like it and so it must be destroyed!"

She stopped for breath and then she whispered, "Kerrel was right about letting an outsider in. And I'm ashamed that I have loved you!"

She turned from him and went swiftly along the gallery. There was a purpose about the way she did it that made Trehearne uneasy. He followed her and found her at the visiphone. The screen was already brightening.

She looked at him with blazing eyes. "I fought once to get you into Llyrdis. Now I'll undo that mistake!"

He struck her away from the instrument and closed the switch. She was on him then like a cat, clawing him, calling him mongrel and freak and worse names, raging at his ingratitude. She was hard to hold but he held her and she could reach neither the visiphone nor the bell to call her servants.

He held her, and she laughed her mocking laugh at him. "All right. Go on, then. Go and make a fool of yourself, trying to free Edri. See how far you get. And remember that it's bad enough for a Vardda born to betray his people but for you—"

He held her a moment longer, swallowing his own rage, thinking. He could not let her go. The moment he left she would send out the alarm, denounce him to the Council, put an end both to his own freedom and to any remote hope he might have of helping Edri.

It took him only a few seconds to decide. In the mood he was in, it was not difficult to strike the necessary, carefully-calculated blow.

He carried her out to the car in his arms. If any of the servants saw them it would look very sweet, very romantic, her dark head on his shoulder, her arms around his neck. They would not be able to see that her wrists were tied.

112

He put her down gently in the padded seat. She did not stir. There was the shadow of a bruise already forming on her chin. He got in beside her and sent the car humming down the wide road that led to the city.

When he was far enough away from the tower he stopped. He bound Shairn securely with strips torn from her own garments, taking especial care with the gag. He arranged her on the floor as comfortably as he could, out of sight. Then he drove on and did not stop again until he reached the spaceport.

The lights were still on in the office of Joris. Probably he would stay late tonight, to oversee the business of taking Edri away in the prison ship. Trehearne felt guilty about Joris, almost as though he were betraying his own father. The old man had been good to him.

Shairn seemed to be safely unconscious. Trehearne left the car where it would be least likely to attract attention, and went into the Administration Building. He had only the vague beginnings of a plan in his mind but whatever he did it would have to start here.

The roar and bustle of the spaceport were not diminished by darkness. Some of the Vardda officers he knew. They hailed him as he passed them in the corridors, congratulating him on his voyage, asking him when he was going out again. Trehearne almost faltered then, thinking what a fool he was to give up all this for an idle hope. And then he remembered Edri and went on. Edri had done his best for him when he needed it, whether it was foolish or not. It seemed that he could not do less for Edri.

The lift took him up to the high room that was like the bridge of a starship that would never fly. Joris was there. He was quite alone. He had been drinking for some time but he was not drunk. He looked up when Trehearne came in and his eyes were heavy and rimmed with red.

"What do you want?" he said.

"A favor."

"Another time, Trehearne. Get out. Get the hell out."

"Another time won't do." Trehearne leaned over the table. "They're taking Edri out for Thuvis tonight. I want to say good-bye to him, Joris. That's all, just a word before he goes. Tell me what ship it is and where

113

—or if you can't do that tell me what sector and I'll see him outside the gate."

"That's right," said Joris. "You're a friend of Edri's." He reached for the wine bottle. There was an empty one beside it and another on the floor. "How good a friend, Trehearne? That's what I'd like to know. How *good* a friend?"

His bloodshot gaze was sharp and very shrewd.

Trehearne said angrily, "You know I'm not mixed up with him. You know where I've been."

"Yes, I know. You've been watching a young boy die in space. What did you think when you saw that, Trehearne? How did you feel?"

"Let's not talk about that," said Trehearne harshly. "Tell me where I can see Edri and when. That isn't much to ask, Joris, just a minute to say good-bye."

"A boy sixteen," whispered Joris, "full of hope, full of longing, proud of his strength . . . I ought to hate you, Trehearne. You're not even half Vardda in the ordinary way and yet you can fly the stars."

He filled his glass again and emptied it. His hands were steady. He was neither drunk nor maudlin. And yet there were tears in his eyes. Trehearne saw them and was somehow shocked. It did not seem possible that Joris could weep.

"Joris," he said gently, "forget about the boy. Let me see Edri."

Again the red-rimmed leaden gaze locked with his, weighing, measuring. "I like you, Trehearne. So I'll tell you again. Get out. Go away. Forget you ever came here."

Trehearne did not move. Abruptly Joris picked up the empty bottle and flung it, not at him but near him. "Get out, you fool! I'm giving you a chance to go!"

There was nothing to do but obey. Trehearne moved toward the door, thinking angrily that he would have to risk the sector map in Operations. He stretched out his hand to the latch and the door opened under it fast and he was looking straight into the prism lens of a shock tube, held by a tall spaceport guard. Shairn was beside the guard.

The guard said, "Back up."

Trehearne backed. He looked at Shairn. "I should have clipped you again to make sure."

"You should. I got my feet loose quite easily. This silk is pretty flimsy stuff." She walked past him toward Joris. The guard came in and closed the door, setting his back against it.

Joris demanded, "What's all this about?"

"I found her out by the gate," the guard said. "She was gagged and her hands were tied."

"Trehearne," said Shairn to Joris. "He's an Orthist. He came here to help Edri escape."

"Did he!" said Joris. "Did he now!" he looked at Trehearne. "You stand where you are. Don't try anything." He reached into a drawer of the table and covered him with the lens of another tube.

"An Orthist, eh?" he said softly. He began to laugh.

XVI

SHAIRN SAT DOWN ON THE EDGE OF JORIS' TABLE. SHE smiled at Trehearne and in this moment he hated her. He looked from Joris to the guard and back again and did nothing. There was nothing then that he could do.

"Would you have believed it of him, Joris?" said Shairn. "Would you have thought that he could turn on us after all we did for him?"

Joris leaned back in his chair. "Shairn," he said, "I'm sorry it had to be this way."

"Yes," she answered, and then added bitterly, "Kerrel was right about him, after all."

Joris said, "That isn't what I mean."

Something in his tone made Shairn turn and look at him. He went on. "I'm sorry you got yourself into this. You're only doing what you believe to be right. But so is Trehearne. *So am I.*"

He dropped his bombshell so quietly that for a moment neither Shairn nor Trehearne could quite believe that they had understood him.

Shairn got up off the edge of the table. She backed away, her eyes fixed on Joris in horrified incredulity. "You, Joris! You an Orthist!" Her tone made the words a denial.

But Joris nodded and said, "Yes."

Abruptly, Trehearne laughed. Shairn swung around. "You heard?" she said to the guard. "Arrest Joris!"

The guard shook his head and smiled. "Hardly. I'm Joris' man."

It was Shairn's turn now to stand like a trapped thing, searching for escape and not finding it.

Trehearne said, "May I move now?" His voice was a bit shaky with relief.

Joris grinned. "I didn't want you throwing yourself around. Somebody might have got hurt. Yes, you can move."

Shairn burst out. "I can't understand this, Joris! You, of all people—it's insane!"

"Perhaps. But I think Trehearne would understand." He scowled at his own hands, brooding, and then he said, "It doesn't matter who knows now. I did the forbidden thing. I married a woman of another world, a non-Vardda. I had a son. He wanted to fly the stars. He used to beg me to take him aboard my ship. After all, he was my son, half-Vardda. He thought he could do it. He hid himself away in my cabin—the Vardda blood had not bred true in him." He glanced briefly at Trehearne. "He was not quite eighteen. I never flew another voyage after that."

He got up, kicking the empty bottle away. "I guess that was why I first gave Trehearne his chance. It seemed to make up in a way for—"

He broke off abruptly. "Well, that's over and done with. We have other things to think about and not much time to do it in. Trehearne, you've upset my plans rather badly by fetching in Miss Spitfire here."

"It wasn't intentional." He went to Joris. "Is it true then? You're going to get Edri free?"

"I'm going to try. You see, this is a thing I could only do once. I've had to sit here for years, watching more than one good man go out to Thuvis, waiting—waiting for the time when I could make my action really count. Now it's here." He turned and glowered at Shairn. "The main question is—what are we going to do with you?"

She answered him angrily and without fear. "Whatever you do, you'll live to regret it!"

"H'm," said Joris. "Tie her up again, Trehearne."

He did so with immense pleasure. This time he used stouter bonds and took extra pains with the knots.

Joris paced up and down, thinking hard. "I hate to say this but there's only one place I know of where there's no danger of her being found before we're gone. And that's aboard the ship."

The guard said, "There won't be any time to get her off again."

"I know it," said Joris grimly. "So it looks as though we'll have an extra passenger."

Trehearne had finished with the gag. He looked at Shairn. Her eyes burned and her face was white above the cloth.

Joris threw his cloak over her. "Take her down in my private lift," he told the guard. "The sector has already been cleared, so you won't have any trouble there. Get her aboard and make damned sure she's locked in."

The guard nodded. He picked up the cloak-wrapped bundle and put it over his shoulder. The buzzer of the visiphone made a sudden jarring sound. Joris motioned the man to hurry, waited until he was gone before answering. Trehearne pressed himself back against the wall, out of range of the screen.

Kerrel's voice said, "Joris—we're bringing Edri down in exactly fifteen minutes. Is everything ready?"

Joris nodded. "The sector is cleared, the guards are posted and the ship is ready for take-off."

"Good. There's a good bit of feeling about this business and we don't want any trouble."

"I've seen to it," Joris told him.

The screen went dark. "The swine!" said Joris. "He's only doing what he believes is right but he's so bloody smug about it. Agent of the Council! Bah!"

Unexpectedly he caught Trehearne's shoulders in a bearlike grip that nearly broke them.

"I'm glad you're with us. Are you armed?"

117

"Yes."

"Come on, then. This is the end of my waiting. I'm going back to space, Trehearne! I'm going to do the things I knew I'd have to do some day after I watched my son die. Come on then—move!"

They went down in the tiny private lift and out of the building to a guarded sector where the lights burned brightly over silent ships, where there were no swarming mobs of non-Vardda workmen, no clatter of machinery and whizzing of busy trams, only the deserted aprons of the great docks and the empty spaces between them.

As they went Joris told Trehearne what he had to do. "Only the guards at the gate, and the four who will pick up Kerrel's men when they come through belong to me. The others, we hope, will be too far away to interfere. But we'll have no time to linger."

"Where is the prison ship?"

"I spotted that at the far end of the sector. And they'll find its generators shot when they try to follow us. The Orthists are strong among the non-Vardda. The mechanics were glad to do that little job for me!"

Joris spoke briefly to the guards about Trehearne. They nodded a welcome. "In about ten minutes," Joris said. "Is the girl aboard?"

"All secure, sir."

"Good. Come along, Trehearne." He led the way past two of the towering docks. By the time they reached the third they were out of sight and hearing of the gate. In this third dock was a long rakish starship, lightless and silent, all hatches closed except the port.

"The *Mirzim,* the ship we're taking," said Joris. "A long-distance light trader, built for speed. Well, we'll need that. It belongs, by the way, to a good friend of mine. He'll have to collect from the two good cargo-ships I'm leaving behind." He added, "The crew's waiting inside now. Only half-crew really—not many navigators and technicians are dependable Orthists."

He stationed Trehearne in the shadows under the corner of the apron. "We'll jump them right here. Try not to kill anyone. As soon as Edri is free make for the *Mirzim.*"

"Right." Trehearne settled back into the patch of darkness, hidden from anyone walking past in the area-

118

way. He held his shock tube ready in his hand. Joris was already gone, heading back to the gate.

Trehearne listened to the sounds of the spaceport. The sharp smell of the sea was in the wind, and in the distance he could see the shining towers of the city. He thought that this was probably the last time he would ever see Llyrdis. He knew a stabbing pang of regret. And then, coming from the direction of the gate, he heard the rhythmic tramp of perhaps a dozen men, moving at a brisk pace toward him. He was glad that the wait was no longer.

He did not move but his body quivered, settling itself.

There was Joris, walking first with Kerrel. There were four men without uniforms. There was a fifth man and beside him Edri, with his right wrist linked to the man's left. There were four men without uniforms, then four of Joris' guards.

The head of the little column passed the corner of the third dock. The four guards broke rank and pulled out their shock tubes, aiming the pallid beams at an angle to avoid hitting Edri.

Trehearne sprang out and joined them.

Three of Kerrel's men went down on that first assault. Two were unconscious but one could still use his shocker. Joris had caught Kerrel unawares and knocked him down with nothing more than his great hammer of a fist. He pulled out his own weapon then and waded in.

A vicious dogfight began, swirling around with Edri as its center. Edri grappled with his guard and they fell, both struggling, both hampered by the fetters.

Both sides quit using the shockers. The fighting was too close for that, a small blundering nasty melee of fists and feet, men stumbling over each other, hitting the wrong people in their haste, going down, getting up again, shouting for help, swearing, astonished, furious.

Trehearne, trying to get to Edri, smashed one man solidly in the face and sent another staggering. Then he was tripped and was kicked as he went down. He found himself sprawling on top of Edri, who grunted and struck at him, then said, "Oh, it's you. The key is in his belt."

Trehearne chopped down with his fist. The man's head rang on the concrete. He lay still and Trehearne found the key. Then a heavy weight descended on him from behind, grinding his face into the cement. The hand that held the key was pinioned in an iron grip. He thrashed about, trying to unseat his attacker, and in the meantime Edri had grabbed his hand as well, wrenching and clawing with a single-minded determination to have the key.

He got it. Trehearne managed to get his knees under him and roll. He saw Kerrel's face close to his. In a second the two men had each other by the throat. They strained together, breast to breast, like two lovers, kicked and tramped by the feet of other men, oblivious. Edri got free and rose. He would have struck Kerrel but Trehearne gasped, "No! I'll handle him!"

Kerrel smiled, an anguished baring of the teeth. His thumbs bit hard into Trehearne's neck. Trehearne let go of Kerrel's throat. He bunched his two fists together and struck upward. Kerrel's head snapped back. His hands loosened. Trehearne tore them away. He threw himself on top of Kerrel. He hit him hard in the face until Kerrel's head rolled like the head of a dead man.

Hands grasped him and tried to drag him away. He shook them off. Kerrel moaned and turned on his side. Trehearne kicked him with his sandalled feet. "That's for Yann," he grunted. "That's for the hounds and for Torin."

A voice roared at him. "Leave it, damn you! Leave it!" A very strong arm thrust him aside. He recognized Joris. There were distant sounds of shouting, coming closer. Kerrel's men were down or scattered. Their own men were running for the *Mirzim,* dragging with them several who were stunned or partly paralyzed. Edri, with a bleeding face, was capering joyously and yelling at him to hurry.

Trehearne shook his head to clear it. He ran beside Joris, stumbling up the metal stair to the apron. He was the last one through the port. Joris hauled down a lever and the port closed and locked itself automatically with a squeal of compressed air.

Instantly the lights went on. The great generators jarred to life. Joris strode heavily down the long corridor to the bridge with Trehearne at his heels. There was another man sitting there but Joris took over the pilot chair.

Trehearne waited tensely but Joris did not touch the controls. He merely sat there, inspecting his bruised fists.

"What the hell are you waiting for?" Trehearne cried. "We've only got a few moments at most!"

Joris looked at him stolidly. "We've only got one life too. We can throw it away by starting at the wrong moment and colliding with incoming ships. I know the dispatch-schedules. Wait."

Trehearne waited. He could not hear inside the ship but he knew that by now alarms must be shrilling all over the spaceport. It was mad to wait. It was craven surrender. Better to run any risk of suicidal collision than to wait . . .

And still Joris waited, an eye cocked on the chronometers, until through the window Trehearne saw lights flashing up outside and men running. And then he glimpsed the loom of a great ship slanting down out of the sky, over and past them.

Joris grunted, suddenly punched the controls. "Hang on!"

The *Mirzim* went up in a screaming arc that crumpled Trehearne to the deck. He clung to a stanchion and prayed that Joris had not lost his skill.

He had not. Even the Vardda flesh had limits. So did metal and the bones of ships. Joris knew to the fraction exactly how much they could stand. The course had already been calculated. He cleared the system, found his coordinates, then hammered the signal relays to the generator rooms. The whine of the generators rose and the needle on the acceleration master dial rose with it. Trehearne watched with bulging eyes, gasping under the pressure, barely restraining an impulse to scream. The second officer was clutching his chair, his face white.

Joris watched the dial. At the precise instant he punched the relay bars again. The needle ceased to blur in its frantic ascent, climbing now with a decent deliberation.

Joris turned around. He looked at his companions and shook with laughter. He had, for the first time since

121

Trehearne had known him, the face of a completely happy man.

Trehearne staggered up. He got out a handkerchief and wiped his face. There was blood on it as well as sweat. "Well," he said, "we're off. But if you don't mind telling me now, Joris—where the devil are we off to?"

"H'm," said Joris. "This may seem a little peculiar to you in view of all the circumstances—"

He roared again with hearty mirth.

"I'll tell you, Trehearne. We're off to Thuvis."

XVII

TREHEARNE STARED AT JORIS. A SMALL TRICKLE OF blood ran from his nose down over his lip. He forgot to wipe it away.

"You're joking," he said.

"Not at all." It was Edri who answered. He had come into the bridge behind Trehearne. He cried good-naturedly, "Blast you, Joris, what are you trying to do—kill us all before we get started?"

"They'll be after us soon enough," said Joris. "We need all the edge we can get."

Trehearne demanded, "Why are we going to Thuvis?"

"Partly," said Edri soberly, "to rescue the men who are rotting away out there. But chiefly because we must have Arrin. You see, Trehearne, he was arrested before he could finish his calculations. When I tried to carry on I added a good bit of my own material—but the missing factor isn't there. Arrin knows it. He must or he couldn't have gone as far as he did. Now if we put our knowledge together—" Edri sighed. "It's been a long, long fight. A thousand years of piecing together lie and legend and hearsay, of hunting down scraps of letters and secret reports, of dredging through tons of irrelevant nonsense in search of one little bit of truth. The Vardda authorities of that day suppressed or destroyed all evidence connected with that last voyage of Orthis. They did their work well. Until now no one has even known in what general sector of the galaxy that last pursuit took place."

He brooded. "Yes, a long fight. And if we're wrong it means the end of hope in our generation. Others will have to begin the search all over again."

It seemed a cruel question to ask but Trehearne could not keep from it.

"Is there any proof that Orthis' ship still exists at all?"

"No. We only know that it was not destroyed at the time that Orthis outran his pursuers and disappeared. For as I told you, long afterward one of the life-skiffs of his ship was picked up in space, with his defiant last message to the galaxy in it."

Edri paused, then added, "Do you wonder that we venerate such a man?"

"I think," said Trehearne slowly, "that you have his kind of courage."

"Maybe." Edri laughed. "I do know that I have a most colossal thirst. You didn't forget the wine stores, Joris?"

"The gods forbid!"

"Let's go and drink." Edri took Trehearne's arm. "And you can tell me a story—where you came from and what in hell you're doing here!"

"No," said Trehearne, without relish. "I think I better see about Shairn."

Edri's jaw dropped. "Shairn?"

"Yes, unfortunately—Shairn." He explained rapidly how the unwilling extra passenger had come aboard.

Edri said some low, hard words. "That isn't going to help matters one little bit. We can hardly leave her on Thuvis and we can't stop anywhere else."

"It couldn't be helped," growled Joris.

"No. Well, I think I'll go with you, Trehearne. I don't believe you'd be safe alone!"

They found her, locked in an officer's cabin for which, on this short-handed trip, there was no officer. She was still bound and gagged. From the look she gave them Trehearne thought she would have killed them both if she had the power.

He freed her. She sat up on the bunk, rubbing her wrists. Two red marks ran from the corners of her mouth across her white cheeks where the gag had rubbed. It gave her a comical expression, like the mask of a clown. There was nothing comical about her eyes.

She did not speak.

Trehearne said awkwardly, "Shairn, I'm sorry about all this. But you might as well make the best of it now you're here."

Still she did not speak. She only sat and looked at him.

Edri said, "Come on, Shairn. A glass of wine will do you good."

She ignored him. Silence and the green deadly eyes, fixed on Trehearne.

He went to her and put his hand on her shoulder. "Be reasonable, Shairn. I know how you feel but none of it was done with intent. And we're all your friends, whether you agree with us or not."

He jerked back but not quite in time. Her claws raked his cheek. He stepped away. She sat motionless and said not one word.

Trehearne swung on his heel and went out. Edri came after him and locked the door. "Perhaps Joris can talk to her," he said. His tone did not hold much hope.

"Oh, she'll come out of it," said Trehearne. "Nobody can stay that mad forever."

Edri shook his head. "I've known her longer than you have. I wouldn't count on it."

The intercom boomed over their heads—Joris calling from the bridge.

"Edri—will you and Trehearne step up here? The bad news is starting to come in."

Communications was just abaft the bridge. Joris had relinquished the controls to the Second and was standing in the cramped space behind the operator, listening intently to the thin metallic voice that came from the ultra-wave receiver.

124

*"Channel one—Alert. All ships in Sector M29 . . .
request radar confirmation on ship believed on course
as follows . . ."*

"Port radar base would have got our coordinates at
take-off, of course," said Joris. "They're just making
sure."

"Listen," said Edri.

The metallic voice finished repeating the coordinates.
It went on, *"All ships will identify immediately when
challenged. All ships will identify . . ."*

"Cruisers," said Edri.

Joris frowned. "They could man at least one in a hurry. I told you we'd need a head start."

He returned to the bridge to inspect the dials and order the generators stepped up.

"We'll have to reach acceleration peak in half the
normal time or we might as well have stayed on Llyrdis.
I'm going to see what radar has turned up."

Trehearne followed along, brooding on the subject of
cruisers. The Vardda had no warships, being in the en-
viable position of having no use for them. But the Council maintained a small fleet of armed craft with maximum velocities considerably above those of the slower
cargo ships, for the purpose of keeping down occasional
outbursts of illegal trading among the Vardda themselves, and for protection of their factors on dangerously
barbaric worlds.

The three-dimensional radar screens showed the normal number of tiny red sparks—the faster-than-light energy impulses of ships' generators. Joris scanned them with
a practised eye.

"Nothing to bother us yet. Too early to tell—the sector immediately behind us is too crowded with shipping
from the port." He turned to Quorn, the Communications officer. "Keep a damn sharp lookout astern. Call
me the minute you see anything unusual. We can spell
you a bit but you're going to get blasted little relief."

Relief was a problem on that voyage. No one got
much of it. They had slightly over half the number of
men required for a full crew under normal circumstances and some of them were not trained technicians.
Trehearne found himself doing one eight-hour trick on
the bridge, calling out dial readings, and another in

Communications. Since, obviously, there was no sending to be done, he could handle the receiver well enough to get by.

Channel One, which was the official, top-priority voice of the Vardda Council, continued to request—and get—confirmation of their course.

It was not long before Quorn reported that radar showed a red spark astern that seemed to be following their course.

Calculating distance by intensity it was possible to judge the rate of approach. Joris demanded more thrust from the generators, ignoring the shuddering agony of the hull and the equally painful reactions of his men.

"Until we pick up Arrin," he said, "it's got to be cut and run. Thuvis is the first place they'll block off, and anything but a direct course on our part will give them time to do it."

They reached their acceleration peak—maximum stress for the fabric of the ship. Joris pushed it over. They prayed.

The observation port began to show a thinning starfield ahead. Wider and wider the areas of darkness spread and the colonies of suns were fewer and more scattered. The red sparks on the radar screens dwindled and faded until two or three were left—lonely traders, outbound to these isolated systems. Those—and the single spark that brightened always astern.

The hours became a lagging monotony of constant watching, constant strain. Numb from lack of sleep, Trehearne went mechanically through his duties, forgot even to worry about what was going to happen. Yesterday was an eon ago, tomorrow was lost in nothingness. There was only today and he was tired.

It was the same with all of them. Joris seemed neither more nor less exhausted than the rest and Trehearne marvelled at the old man's strength.

Shairn remained locked in her cabin. She would not speak to anyone, except the youngster who brought her food, then only to voice a curt thanks.

Ahead the darkness deepened. The main axis of the Milky Way plane was "below" them. Beyond the isolated systems they could glimpse the lightless gulf of utter emptiness. Its black blankness afflicted Trehearne with a creeping horror. It was like seeing the primal Chaos before creation.

At last a dim red sun was centered in the field. It began to grow. The radar screens were empty, save for the one grim following spark that had become almost a flame, ominously bright.

Joris made his calculations and again they prayed.

They completed deceleration in a little less than half the normal time. That was the period during which no one ate and only those who had to remained erect.

Thuvis hung in the sky before them, an idiot sun, devouring the last of its strength and peering with a dull red eye at the cosmic face of death. It was circled by a single world.

"We'll have to make it fast," said Joris harshly. "You be ready, Edri."

The *Mirzim* landed on an arid tableland swept by bitter winds. Quorn stayed to maintain his tense vigil at the radar screens but the rest of them went out, glad of solid ground if only for a few minutes.

The wind-driven dust tore at Trehearne, cutting into his flesh like tiny cold daggers. The sky was dusky at midday but there were few stars. Even at night there would be few stars here. The sullen glare of Thuvis washed the dusty desert world with red and where a deep ravine cleft the tableland the shadows clung like clotted blood. Trehearne could not think of a place that more resembled hell.

Edri had hastened to the lip of the ravine. Trehearne followed and looked down. Below the steep sides, below the ugly screes, was a tangle of pallid vegetation, stunted trees and leprous shrubbery, clustered around warm springs that smoked like little fumaroles in the chill air. There was a settlement here, three or four small plastic structures surrounded by a wall, and outside the wall a pathetic expanse of tilled land.

"They're coming!" cried Edri. "They saw the ship . . ."

A narrow path led steeply up from the ravine. Men were already toiling along it. Trehearne counted them. Eight, ten, eleven—eleven men, the total population of this world of ultimate exile.

Edri was shouting. His voice echoed back and forth

in the ravine with a hollow booming sound. Other shouts answered him. The men on the path began to run. They slipped and staggered in their haste, clawing their way upward. Trehearne could see their white faces strained toward him.

He watched them come—gaunt wind-bitten hopeless men with the greyness of living death upon them, striving up from that deep red-lit prison, answering the call of Edri's voice. He saw their eyes, the eyes of men called back suddenly from that terrible numbing of the mind that is worse than clean destruction.

Edri threw his arms around the man who came first over the rim. He had not been there as long as the others and the stamp was not so deep on him. He turned and shouted at his mates to hurry. His beard and his unkempt hair blew in the wind and his voice was wild.

Edri cried to him, "No time for talk now, Arrin! Is that all of you?"

It was. The line of bearded scarecrows hastened toward the *Mirzim*. Ready hands helped them in.

The voice of Quorn yelled over the intercom, "They're right on top of us! Hurry it up!"

Joris had thrust his way forward to the bridge. He was at his station and waiting before the port was closed.

"Ready for take-off! Watch yourselves!"

His hand reached out for the signal relays. And then Trehearne saw it hesitate and fall back.

From the opening door of the Communications room another voice spoke, perfectly audible at that short distance—the metallic voice of the receiver.

"We have your range. Do not attempt to take off. We have your range. Do not attempt. . . ."

Over Joris' suddenly shrunken shoulders, through the bridge port, Trehearne saw the long slim shape of a cruiser sweep in toward a landing close beside them.

XVIII

KERREL'S FACE APPEARED ON THE SMALL SCREEN. There was no need now for the ultra-wave and the ordinary visiphone unit had been cut in. Edri and Joris confronted him. Trehearne stood in the doorway, listening. Behind him were the rescued exiles, and black despair was on them all.

Kerrel regarded Edri and Joris with a weary hatred. He seemed to have learned that being an agent of the Council had its rough side. But there was no slightest hint of leniency in his tone.

"The gun crew has orders to open fire in exactly fifteen minutes," he said. "You have that long to clear your ship, bringing with you neither weapons nor personal gear of any sort." He repeated, "Fifteen minutes precisely."

Joris looked at him with red and sunken eyes. Twenty years of age had come upon him in the last few minutes. He could not seem to bring himself to speak. Edri's hands were clenched so tightly that the fingers were bone white. They moved back and forth, seeking something to strike and not finding it. He too had become old.

"Fourteen minutes," said Kerrel, without emotion. "You're wasting time."

Edri turned abruptly and thrust his way blindly past Trehearne, who caught and held him in the doorway.

"Let go," said Edri viciously and cursed him. "That ravine is deep. I can step off into it now as well as later. I won't be taken back."

"Hold on," said Trehearne. A sudden wild hope had

129

come to him. He lifted his voice. "Kerrel! Kerrel, can you hear me?" He was out of visual range of the screen.

"Yes, Trehearne, I hear you."

"Then listen! Tell your men to hold their fire. We have Shairn aboard!"

Joris' head came up sharply. Edri stopped fighting. And in the screen Kerrel's mirrored face went through the shadings of surprise, shock, then understanding and a wry mirth.

"You have a quick mind, Trehearne," he said. "But it won't do. Thirteen minutes."

"Go and get her, Edri," said Trehearne. His mouth was dry, his body drenched with cold sweat.

Edri plunged away into the corridor. Trehearne went and stood where Kerrel could see him. He smiled and wondered if Kerrel could hear the knocking of his heart against his ribs. Joris stood motionless, waiting. Kerrel counted off the minutes, and at each count his voice became more strained, his eyes less certain.

There were six minutes left when Edri came back with Shairn and thrust her in front of the screen.

"You see?" said Trehearne. "I wasn't lying."

Kerrel forgot to count. He stared at the girl, the strong lines of his face crumbling into indecision. He said her name once. Suddenly he turned and was gone from the screen. They could hear him shouting somewhere beyond, "Hold your fire! Hold your fire! They have a prisoner aboard."

Trehearne knew then that he had not misjudged the depth of the other's passion. And strangely that knowledge was bitter to him.

Kerrel came into view again, and Shairn cried out, "Kerrel, they're after something more than these Orthist exiles! I think they're—"

Trehearne put his hand over her mouth. "It doesn't matter what she thinks. The important thing is her life. How much is it worth to you, Kerrel?"

Kerrel ran his hand nervously over his face and did not answer at once. Trehearne kept his palm firmly on Shairn's mouth.

Kerrel shook his head. "You wouldn't kill her, Trehearne."

130

"No, I wouldn't," Trehearne answered. "But I'm only one and there are others aboard. Eleven men of Thuvis, who feel that one life is very little to pay for escape from this hell-hole. Come on, Kerrel, how much is Shairn worth to you? You can have her—free, clear and alive."

Kerrel asked, "What do you want?"

"A head start."

"It won't do you any good. You can't outrun a cruiser."

Joris said, "We'll take that chance!"

Again Kerrel hesitated. "What are your terms?"

Trehearne said, "You will allow us to take off and we'll guarantee to land Shairn safely on the other side of this planet. You will keep your ship here until you receive our message that that has been done. We will both be able to check each other's actions by radar and if your generators are started before our second take-off we'll know it."

Kerrel thought, and then asked sullenly, "What assurance have I that you will actually release her?"

"You can take my word for that," Trehearne told him. "Either that or blow her to bits with the rest of us."

There was another long tense moment of silence. And then Kerrel said, "All right." He spoke the words as though they had a taste of vitriol on his tongue.

Joris was out of Communications in one long stride.

Kerrel looked at Shairn and cried, "Wait! You must radio your position when you set her down."

"We will."

Trehearne flipped the switch. The screen went blank. The throbbing generators took the ship and lifted it and whirled it away and no gun spoke from the cruiser. Trehearne released his grip on Shairn. Reaction and relief had turned his knees to water, so that it was difficult to stand against the lurching of the ship.

Shairn turned and looked at him. "You're a fool, Michael," she said, "but I'll give you this. You're not a coward."

He had her locked in her cabin again and went back to the bridge. Joris was scowling at the projection of the microfilm chart of the planet.

"There," he said, and pointed to a huge emptiness.

"She'll be safe there until they pick her up—there's no predatory life in these deserts." He glanced up at Trehearne. "Good man," he said. "Me, I was beaten."

Trehearne gave him a wry smile. "Me, I bluffed. From here on, Joris, it's all yours. Where's Edri?"

"Shut in his cabin with Arrin. They know the general sector, clear out at the galaxy's edge. Now they're trying to figure out the true course together." And Joris snorted. "Course! If I can keep one jump ahead of that cruiser I'll be satisfied."

The *Mirzim* skimmed over the darkling world of Thuvis into the starless night. Trehearne sat and brooded, thinking of Shairn, thinking of the two men who were bent over the final calculations of a dream that had balked men for a thousand years. He thought of what a dream can do to a man, of how far it can lead him away from the good safe life of common sense to the ultimate voids of creation. He hoped that Edri and Arrin would find what they wanted. He hoped they would live to find it.

"Coming down," said Joris. "Better get Shairn a coverall. It's cold down there."

Trehearne found a warm coverall in the equipment locker and took it to Shairn's cabin. She put it on, and he saw how her face was shadowed with weariness and strain.

She said quietly, "Do you still love me, Michael?"

Her question took him by surprise, and the answer came of itself. "Yes," he said. "Yes, I do."

"Then we must stop behaving like two angry children and not throw away the life we can have together."

He bent his head. "I'm sorry you got caught in this."

"It's as much my fault as yours. I was too quick to lose my temper. I should have stopped to think that the Vardda world was so new to you that you had little to judge it by."

She was not now the mocking Shairn of old. Her voice was full of a sombre passion, a pleading for him to understand.

"Michael, your motives were good—loyalty to a friend, reaction against what seemed to you injustice. But surely now you must see how hopeless this all is. I know you're hunting Orthis' ship. You'll never reach it.

Kerrel will run you down. It'll all have been for nothing."

It seemed to Trehearne that what she said was very likely true. But he only answered, "It's too late to think about that now."

"No, Michael! You can still save yourself!" She caught him by the shoulders, her hands urgent on his flesh. "Leave the ship with me! Let Kerrel pick us both up!"

Trehearne smiled mirthlessly. "Kerrel would like that —taking me back to a prison."

"It doesn't have to be prison!" Shairn exclaimed. "You can say you pretended to join Joris and Edri only to save me. I'll back you up and not Kerrel nor anyone else can disprove it. You'll walk out free on Llyrdis."

It crossed his mind that he could do that. It would all fit. It was an out.

"You won't be letting your friends down, either," Shairn insisted. "They'll go on without you. You've done all you can for them."

She clung to him. Her mouth begged him with a silent language of its own. He took her arms slowly from around him and thrust her back and she caught her breath at the pain of his grip.

"No," he said. And again, "No, Shairn."

She stood back and looked at him steadily. "You could go back to the Silver Tower with me but you won't—and for what? So that peoples you've never met on worlds you'll never see can someday fly the stars?"

"There was a man named Trehearne on the world Earth who got his chance to fly the stars," he said. "I thought that others should have their chance too. I have to play it out now."

She was silent and then the dropping speed of the ship told them that it was almost over. Trehearne took her down to the airlock chamber. They stood there together, not finding anything more to say, and all that had been between them came silently and mocked them with the pain of vanished days.

The *Mirzim* scraped her keel softly on a yielding surface and was still. Trehearne opened the port, looking out on the dark windy desert.

Shairn spoke then. "A strange beginning for us, Michael, and now an even stranger ending."

He held out his hand to help her down and the pressure of her fingers was like something tearing at his heart. She looked up at him, a small lonely figure in the vast dark. He thought her lips moved but the wind came between them and took the words away and he had none of his own for answer.

The warning bell jarred harshly in his ears. He closed the port and she was gone.

Joris' voice roared from the bridge through the intercom. "Flatten out, all! This is the only start we'll get on Kerrel and I've got to pile it on!"

The cruel hand of acceleration crushed Trehearne down. He lay on the scored plates of the deck and that last vision of Shairn's white face remained with him to remind him of all that he had had and lost.

He said her name over and over in the silence of the empty lock and his mouth was filled with the bitter taste of dust. The *Mirzim* leaped through space like a wild thing, driving toward the sector that was the goal of a thousand-year hope and quest, toward the galaxy edge and the shores of outer night.

XIX

THEY HAD STEPPED CLEAR OUT TO THE EDGE OF THE galaxy, where the fringing stars were lost in the outer void and the dead suns swept forever through the entombing dark, where even the memory of creation was gone, blotted out by unimaginable time. No delimited frontier was here, but a border region between the swarming star-sparks and the black abyss beyond.

Trehearne tried to remember how long it had been

since they had taken off from Thuvis. He couldn't. Time seemed oddly elastic when you lost all the familiar frames of reference. He gave it up. It didn't matter. He peered with aching bloodshot eyes into the lightless seas that lie beyond the island universes and tried to remember why he had come here. And that too was dim in his mind.

Edri was bent over a table that had been set up in the bridge. He no longer looked like Edri. He seemed to have been working for a million years. Arrin sat near him. He held his head between his bony hands, a bearded mummy embalmed upright, hardly retaining the semblance of life. There were charts under Edri's hands, endless sheets of calculations and graphs, endless miles of figures. Joris studied them, bending beside Edri. His broad jowls hung down now over his wrinkled collar. His eyes had sunk deep under ridges of bone, peering out as from two shadowed caves.

Edri was talking in a voice that came from far away. The words reached Trehearne in droning snatches from beyond the fog of weariness.

"—so our only way to locate Orthis' ship was to triangulate its position from two separate bearings on it. One bearing was the course of that life-skiff Orthis sent in with his last message, allowing for aberrations caused by the gravitational field of stars. The other bearing was Orthis' course in his last flight. We couldn't get that till I found the part of the Lankar manuscript that Arrin didn't have."

Trehearne heard someone ask, "Who was Lankar?"

"One of Orthis' last pursuers, who left a secret log of the pursuit to ease his guilty conscience. Enough of it survived—"

Joris said, "The hell with Lankar. Get on with it."

"We had to push the star-maps back in time— galactic motion, star streaming, a million complicated problems of relative motion and proper motion, back five hundred years and then another five hundred, and then correlate them. Handling an almost unlimited number of variables like that, it could only be done on the biggest math-machines and electronic computers at Llyrdis. And that meant it all had to be done secretly, bit by bit. That work's been going on for a long, long time."

Edri drew a long breath that was coupled with a racking yawn.

"The resultant charts indicate an unnamed dark star following an orbit here, outside the main stream of the galaxy." He traced a line with his finger. "These charts for the fringing stars are incomplete, as you know. There's nothing to draw anyone out to these godforsaken regions and they've never been properly explored. But according to our calculations, that dark star was in the right place a thousand years ago and Orthis' lifeskiff was launched from there. Now the wheel of the galaxy has turned so, taking the dark star with it . . ."

He laid his hand on the crossing of two marked lines on the chart, and looked at them.

"That's our destination, Joris. If we're right, the ship of Orthis is there. If we're wrong—well, somebody else will have to try again in another thousand years."

He remained standing, silent, his hands braced on the table, too tired to move. Joris rubbed his bleary eyes and began to read the coordinates aloud from the chart. Mechanically the Second Officer set up the combination on the finder.

Joris moved heavily back to the pilot chair. When the finder clicked off the new course, he set the *Mirzim* on it. Then he spoke over the intercom to Radar. "What's the position of that cruiser?"

A croaking voice answered him. He listened, and then turned to the others. "Closer," he said. "Always closer."

Trehearne's mind turned back to its constant half-waking nightmare. The cruiser, following, hanging on, dogged, persistent, relentless. He lived over painfully every maneuver, every trick by which Joris had managed to delay their pursuer, to grasp a little more time, a little more distance.

He remembered the last-minute plunge into a dark nebula when the cruiser was almost close enough to range them. He remembered the turning and twisting and doubling inside the blackness of the cloud, where the absorptive cosmic dust fogged the radar. They had lost the cruiser there. They had got clear away and for a time they had hoped. They had made it to this fringe sector—and then the red spark showed again on the screen, coming closer, always closer.

136

There were times when Trehearne forgot the physical fact of the cruiser, a ship of ordinary metal officered and manned by ordinary Vardda spacemen. At such times it seemed to him that the *Mirzim* was pursued by a demoniac nemesis striding naked across the plunging gulfs —a nemesis wearing Kerrel's face with Kerrel's hands outstretched to grasp them.

Sometimes Shairn's face was there beside Kerrel's, white, unreadable, a misty cloud that blotted out the stars.

The hoarse voice of the radar man croaked at intervals. The ship fled on toward the dark star.

Joris finally turned around. The table had been taken out, the charts and the toilsome calculations rolled up and shoved away. Arrin lay on the deck against the after bulkhead, sleeping. He would not leave the bridge until he knew whether or not his life and work had gone for nothing. Edri sat beside him. He was not asleep.

Joris said flatly, "It isn't going to work."

Edri said nothing. He waited.

Joris went on, as though he hated what he was saying, but had to say it. "Look at it. As soon as I start deceleration the cruiser will begin to cut our lead to nothing. And they're stressed for less deceleration time than I can make without tearing the *Mirzim* to pieces. What'll happen? They'll be down on us before we can even begin our search."

Edri nodded. He leaned back against the bulkhead and closed his eyes. He said, "They know now what we're after. What do you suppose Kerrel would do if he found the ship of Orthis?"

Nobody answered that. There was no need to answer. A heavy silence followed, during which Trehearne thought of the messages that had gone out across the galaxy from the cruiser's ultra-wave—guarded messages that betrayed by their very spareness the desperate nature of this mission, urgent requests for other Council cruisers to close up with all speed. But those others were still too far away to matter. Whatever happened would have happened before they could come up. Kerrel was going to finish this alone.

Edri said, "What are we going to do?"

Joris rubbed his big hand over his stubbled face and

blinked and said, "Our only chance, if Orthis' ship and secret are really there, is to get the ultra-wave equipment to it in time for what we planned." He went on slowly, "I think our life-skiff could carry that equipment. If we drop the skiff it could travel on constant velocity for a while before it would have to decelerate. Meanwhile I could swing the *Mirzim* on another course, running back along the rim of the galaxy, away from the dark star. The cruiser would follow me. Chances are, with their radar concentrated on me to catch my lateral-impulse pattern, they wouldn't notice the skiff at all when she started deceleration."

He sighed. "They'd catch us, of course. But the *Mirzim* isn't going to keep on forever after the beating she's taken. The generators are in bad shape. But we could keep going long enough to give you time."

Edri thought it over. "I don't like it," he said. "But it looks as though it's that or nothing."

Joris was muttering under his breath about maximum loads and capacity. "The main ultra-wave equipment," he said, "and three men. The skiff would keep that. We'd keep the auxiliary ultra-wave set here, of course."

"Who can you spare? You'll need all your flight-technicians."

"He can spare me," said Trehearne. "I'm the most nonessential. And I can still stand up if I have to."

Joris nodded. "Yes. Quorn has to go to handle the ultra-wave, of course—and he can handle the skiff all right."

"Who else?"

"You," said Joris.

Edri looked at the sleeping Arrin. "He ought to go instead of me. He's worked for it longer than I have." It was obvious that Arrin was unable to go anywhere, and Edri sighed. He pulled himself erect. "All right, then. Come on, Trehearne. We'll start loading."

The skiff was contained in a cell of its own, sunk in the side of the *Mirzim*—a miniature star-ship with a flight range long enough to give the crew of a disabled ship a chance to reach safety. But there was no use trying to think of safety any longer.

Trehearne routed out every man that was off-station

138

and could stand erect. Following Edri's orders he stripped the skiff of everything they wouldn't need. Quorn oversaw the removal of the heavy ultra-wave radio equipment from the *Mirzim* and its loading into the skiff. He seemed unnecessarily particular about it. Trehearne swore and sweated but got it done. Then he went back to the bridge with Edri and Quorn. Joris studied his instruments.

"Pretty soon," he said. He gave Quorn his flight instructions. "Trehearne is still a lubber," he remarked, "but he knows enough by now to give you a hand when you need it."

Edri said, "Surrender as soon as you're challenged, Joris."

Joris laughed, a pallid ghost of his old loud roar. "I will. Right now, I'm too tired to die." He glanced again at the instruments. "Time to go."

They looked at each other, these fatigue-drunken red-eyed men whom a dream had dragged to the edge of the universe, and could find nothing to say in this moment of their parting.

"Good luck," muttered Edri then and turned away.

"You're the ones who're going to need it," Joris called after them.

Trehearne went through after Quorn and Edri into the skiff. They sealed off and then Quorn took the controls and waited, watching his chronometer. His hand grasped loosely about a red switch marked RELEASE.

He closed the switch.

There was a squeal and grind of machinery, a sense of super-swift forces at work as the complicated releasing-gear did its work, an instant of extreme pressure, and the skiff had left the *Mirzim*. They could see nothing but they knew that skiff and ship had already diverged far apart at their unthinkable speeds.

Quorn watched his instruments while Trehearne and Edri sat looking at nothing, afraid to sleep lest they should not be able to wake again. They sat, and swayed, and waited, until presently Quorn started his forward generator and began deceleration.

Trehearne lost track of things. Part of the following time he was unconscious, or nearly so. The rest of it he observed as in a confused dream. He thought of how he had once been wildly eager for starflight. But he managed to do the things that Quorn required of him.

The port cleared. It had no adapter and functioned as a port only at visual speeds. Now, ahead of them, Trehearne could see a huge bulk of darkness against the outer dark, illuminated only faintly by the galactic light.

"There it is," said Edri. "The dark star." His voice shook a little.

They swept closer, still slowing down. "It has a planet," said Quorn. "There, catching the starshine——"

"Two," said Trehearne. "I see two."

Two dimly gleaming bodies, dead worlds clinging to a long dead sun out here at galaxy edge. The glow of the Milky Way touched them, the ghostly glow of candles at a wake, and only emphasized their drear darksomeness and lonesomeness.

Edri whispered, "We'll try the outer planet first. Give me a hand, Trehearne."

They crawled aft between the crowded banks of equipment to a detector that had come from the *Mirzim's* hold. Edri fumbled at it.

"In Orthis' day they used radioactive fuel, of course," Edri mumbled. "We calculated its half-life. Even supposing his bunkers were nearly empty there should be enough left to register on this counter. A teacupful would do it."

Trehearne helped Edri adjust the shielding apparatus on the mechanism until the needle was still.

"What about natural radioactive deposits on the planets themselves?" he asked.

"We get a break there. Too old. The last radioactive element will have practically died out millions of years ago." He raised his voice. "Keep the skiff as low as you dare, Quorn. The counter has a wide sweep. Take it slow."

He crouched over the telltale needle. Trehearne moved forward again.

The planet was small, less than two thousand miles in diameter. Between the intense gloom and the motion of the skiff he could see nothing but a black featureless desolation, rifted here and there with white that he took to be the frozen remains of an atmosphere. He thought what it would be like to land there and shivered.

They quartered and swept the planet carefully. The telltale needle of the counter remained motionless. Edri said, heavily, "We'll go on. Pray we find it on the other planet. Pray Orthis didn't come down on the dark star. It would take forever to find him there."

Quorn fed in power and cleared away. The port dimmed again, and Edri moaned.

"He's about out," Quorn said. "Looks like whatever is done, we'll have to do the most of it."

The second world was larger than the first by three times or more. It was not content to be featureless. It thrust up gnawed and shattered ranges, stripped bones of mountains sheathed in frozen gases. It showed forth dreary plains coated white with congealed air, glistening faintly in the light of the great galactic wheel. It turned toward the watchers the naked beds of its vanished oceans, sucked dry to the deepest gulf. It displayed the scars of its long dying, the brutal wounds of internal explosion, the riven gashes of a shrinking crust. A hideous world that seemed to remember beauty still and to resent the cruelty of death.

Edri whispered, "Pray—pray that the damned thing moves." Instead of doing so, he cursed the needle that it did not stir.

"Keep going," said Trehearne.

They kept going.

The needle quivered.

Edri let out a hoarse cry. "Easy! *Easy!*" Tears began to run down his cheeks. He sobbed. The needle was still again.

"Circle!" Trehearne shouted to Quorn. "Circle till we get it centered."

He ran his tongue over his lips and tasted salt, and wondered how it got there.

Quorn swung the skiff around in a tightening spiral until Edri said, "Now! Let her down."

He scrambled forward, thrusting his face against the port, trying to see. Quorn switched on a landing-light. The blue-white blaze lit up a circular area below, the light intensely bright, the shadows intensely black. Its beam went sharply down.

141

They followed it. It was as though the skiff were poised on that pillar of light, sinking downward. They were above a planetary surface racked and tortured by final diastrophism. Towering miles high, loomed a mighty cliff of riven rock. In front of it a chasm yawned, and beyond the chasm a drear and tumbled landscape stretched dim under the great sword of the galaxy.

They started down along the face of the titanic cliff. Looking at the chasm at its base Trehearne began to get uneasy.

"There's no ship here," he said. "The counter must have picked up some last radiation from deep down in that chasm."

Quorn agreed with him. But Edri said, "No, keep going." Trehearne could feel him tremble.

They went on down the face of the giant, looming wall. Trehearne pointed suddenly. "Isn't that a ledge?"

The hard bright edge of the beam cut across a shelf of rock that jutted out halfway down the cliff. Quorn swung the skiff in closer. Something on the ledge glistened dully under the light. Quorn let the skiff drop with a sickening rush. Detail sprang clear—shattered rock, ancient magma, puddles of frozen air in the hollows. And among them an ovoid shape, symmetrical, smooth, giving back a metallic glint.

Edri said the name of Orthis, as though it were a prayer.

XX

QUORN HAD SET THE SKIFF DOWN ON THE LEDGE. THEY had scrambled into pressure suits. They had forgotten that they were already three-quarters dead. Awkward in the clumsy armor, stumbling on the jagged rock, slipping on the patches of frozen air, they clawed their way toward the goal they had crossed a galaxy and gambled their lives to find. Above them the ghastly cliff leaned outward against nothingness, below them the abyss plunged down into the dead heart of a world. Beyond them was a spreading desolation, and in the black sky the awful rim of the galaxy lay like a blazing sword of light.

Trehearne was aware of the silence. He had never been on an airless world before. He felt the impact as his metal boot struck against a shard of rock, but it made no sound. All he could hear was the harsh breathing of Quorn and Edri, transmitted to him by the helmet audio.

The ship of Orthis loomed before them, lightless, lifeless, cradled in the ashes of destruction. It had a look of patience. It had lain here for a thousand years, untouched by time or rust, entombed in silence and the endless night, eternal as the dead suns that rove forever in uncorrupting space. It seemed that it could wait until the end of the universe, cherishing its trust. Awe came upon Trehearne, and with it a kind of fear.

They found the lock port. It stood wide open, the valves still clean and shining. There could be no corrosion here, with every atom of air and moisture frozen in the purifying cold. The light of Trehearne's belt-lamp showed him, on the floor of the lock chamber, the scored marks of a man's boot. They might have been made only yesterday.

The three men paused outside that open port. They looked at each other through the glassite plates of their helmets, and their faces were strange. Then Trehearne stepped aside, and Quorn also. Edri bent his head. He moved forward to the port. Slowly, without sound, he clambered into the ship of Orthis.

The others were close behind him. Their belt lamps cut hard slashes of light across the airless dark. They passed through the lock chamber and came into a corridor running fore and aft. It was utterly still. The heavy drag of their boots on the metal deck made not the slightest sound. It was like walking in a fever-dream, and the deadness of the ship, the black, inert, unstirring deadness, was more oppressive than the desolation in

143

which it lay. The rocks and cliffs had never moved, they had never been built by the hands of men, no thought or hope had ever entered into them. Trehearne's skin crept in little waves of cold. He could hear the beating of his own blood in his ears, the dull throbbing of his own heart. He moved with the others, lonely figures in a tomb, and he started like a child at every shape the light picked out.

The whole after section of the ship was a laboratory. Much of the delicate equipment was shattered, either by speed-vibration or a hard landing. Trehearne could make nothing of the tortured mass of metal and splintered crystal, but Quorn said, very softly, "He was studying interstellar radiation. Most of that stuff is beyond me, but I can see that much."

One section of the laboratory contained a complicated mass of coils and prisms and intricate banks of reflectors arranged around what must have been a great central tube. There was a small platform at the focal point of the mechnism, fitted with straps. Along one bulkhead was a stack of metal cages for experimental animals. Several of the little creatures were still there. They had died, the quick death of airlessness and cold, but their bodies were still perfect. They had, then, survived the voyage. The ultra-speeds of interstellar flight had not harmed them.

The men searched for a time among the wreckage, and then Edri said, "There's nothing for us here. No good trying to figure out the apparatus. They couldn't do that in all the years they had the ship impounded, when it was all in shape. Most of it Orthis designed and built himself."

Trehearne looked again at the small furry bodies in the cages, lying as though in sleep. Somehow they made the betrayal of Orthis doubly cruel—that even beasts could be given the freedom of the stars, that so many generations of the races of so many worlds had been denied.

They went into the corridor, retracing their steps, and passed on forward. They found the living quarters, small and spare and monastically neat. The coverings of the bunk were rumpled and the pillow still retained the hollow where a man's head had lain. Trehearne shivered. Presently they went on, to the bridge.

Trehearne realized then what an act of heroism it had been to push this antique ship to the limits of the galaxy and beyond. The instruments were so few and rudimentary, the system of controls so crude. There was a locking device, a primitive Iron Mike that could keep the ship on its course without human attention, and he thought that only that had made Orthis' lonely flight possible. But the science of star-craft had come a long way since then.

Quorn's voice, held to a whisper as one speaks in a church, reached him on the helmet phone. "It's incredible. This ship wasn't even built for voyaging, it was a spatial laboratory. It's a wonder it survived at all."

Edri drew a long breath, with a quiver in it like a sob. "We still haven't found what we're looking for. Do you suppose it isn't here? Do you suppose that after all . . ." He didn't finish.

They began to search again. It was Trehearne who found the door in the after bulkhead of the bridge. He pushed it open and looked through into the cabin beyond. The beam of his belt-lamp speared brightly into the immemorial dark.

Involuntarily, he screamed.

Quorn and Edri ran to him. He was clinging to the bulkhead. Cold sweat poured down his face, and his eyes were wide and wild. They looked past him, over his shoulder.

The cabin was small. It was fitted as a library, crammed with metal cases of books, some of them microtape volumes of an ancient type, some of them thick ragged notebooks. The knife-sharp light-beams picked them out, in brilliant highlight and black shadow. There was a great table, bolted down, and on the table was a metal box. A man's hand rested there, the fingers open, curled slightly over the edge of the box, protectively, possessively, as though it were something loved and precious.

"Oh God," whispered Quorn, "look at him . . ."

He sat in a metal chair behind the table. His head was lifted, looking toward the port in the outer wall that

145

showed the black sky slashed across with the mighty fires of the galaxy. The hard light showed him clearly. He was an old man. The years of his life had been many and unkind. They had shaped his face as though from iron, gouging the lines deep, hammering the ridges hard, driving out all traces of youth and hope and whatever laughter there might have been to forge a mask of bitter anger, and reproach, and in the end, despair. It seemed to Trehearne that he could read a whole life history in that face, caught forever in the moment of death, when surely the man was crying out upon whatever gods he worshipped, demanding *Why?*

Edri began suddenly to laugh. "Orthis. It's Orthis. He's been here waiting for us to come in . . ."

Quorn raised a hand in its heavy gauntlet and struck Edri's helmet so that Trehearne could hear the ringing in his own audio. "Shut up. Damn you, Edri. Shut up." Edri stopped laughing. After a moment he said, "For a moment I thought . . ."

Trehearne muttered, "So did I." Here in the airless utter cold, death held no decay, no change. But there was more to it than the lack of physical corruption. The fire in this man had burned so deep that even death could not erase its scars. Where the lamp-beams caught them, his open eyes seemed still to glow with the unforgotten embers.

For a long time the three men stood, not moving, grouped in the doorway. Trehearne said once, "I think he wanted whoever found him to look inside that box, there under his hand." Orthis' life-work, the future of the galaxy, held in a little box. They knew it. But still they were not quite ready to go in and take away from Orthis the thing that he had kept so long. And it was strange, Trehearne thought, that in this moment when their emotions ought to be at the highest pitch, when they should be feeling most poignantly the weight of all the centuries of sacrifice and struggle that had led them here, and what it was all going to mean, they were too tired to feel anything very much, only the edges of awe and an instinctive reluctance to approach the dead. He wanted to get away from this funeral ship. Finally he wanted it so much that he went in and tried to move Orthis' hand from off the box. The arm was frozen rigid as

146

a steel bar, and he gave it up, working the box carefully out from under the icy fingers, in horror lest they break.

The others had come slowly in beside him. The box was not locked. He lifted up the lid, and the lamplight showed a notebook bound in cloth. On top of it lay a loose sheet of paper with a few angular lines of writing. Edri picked it up, very clumsily in his armored hands, and held it to the light, reading aloud in a queer flat voice. "I have clung to life this much longer . . ."

Edri stopped, and coughed, and started over, and Trehearne thought that Orthis listened.

"I have clung to life this much longer to write down for the first time all my formulae, complete and simplified so that they can be understood and used. In them lies the freedom of the stars. I, the first of the star-born, was rejected by the greed and fear of the planet-born. But it will not always be so.

"I shall not see what comes. My ship has already flown too far, I have little fuel, and I am old. Therefore I have set the airlock control and in a few minutes it will open. A swift death, and better than a slow one as the air-pumps fail. After that, I shall wait. What I dreamed will never be forgotten. Some day there will come others who believe as I have always believed, that the stars are for all men."

Edri fell silent. And Quorn said, "He watched the galaxy for a thousand years, and waited."

Trehearne forced himself to move, to break the spell. "Unless we hurry, it will not have done him any good." He reached out and took the box and shut it, and thrust it into Edri's hands. "Come on, Edri, do you hear me? Come on! We haven't got much time."

Edri looked at the box, and then at Orthis, who had had a thousand years of time. Then he turned and went out, and Quorn went after him, and Trehearne, down the dark corridor and out of the silent ship. Trehearne looked up at the flaming river of stars in the sky and thought what a mighty dream the first of the star-born men had carried with him into the long night.

A sudden panic of haste came over him. Orthis had given them this trust literally with his own hand. If they failed now because they were too slow, too worn out now, at the last, to do what needed to be done . . . He

147

began to run toward the skiff, shouting at the others, urging them on, harrying them until they ran too, staggering over the blasted rock. He pushed them inside, a little crazy now himself, talking incessantly about the need for haste. Quorn took off from the ledge. They did not want to be near the ship of Orthis when they did what they were going to do. He sent the light craft racing across the dead world, searching for a place to land.

"Hurry," said Trehearne. "Got to hurry!"

Quorn cursed him savagely. "I'm doing all I can. Shut up and listen. Both of you. Keep your pressure suits on and your helmets ready."

Trehearne stopped talking. He sat, holding his hands tight between his knees, shaking all over. Edri was bent over the notebook from the metal box, reading.

"It's all here," he said. His voice was hoarse with weariness, with emotion he was too numb to feel. "The equations, the formulae, the instructions for constructing the equipment, the instructions for using it. I don't understand them, but others will." He looked at Trehearne with red-rimmed eyes. "Orthis has a foreword here. He *was* the first of the star-born. The mutation began spontaneously on that first long voyage. The constant vibration of speed, not speed as we know it now but more than the human body was used to, speed approaching the velocity of light, and the impact of interstellar radiation on the living cell. That's what did it. Orthis was the end-product of four generations of breeding under those conditions. He was nature's first attempt to create Galactic Man, to readjust the human body to meet new needs. And the thing he labored on so long was the reduction of that long natural process to a workable formula that could accomplish the change in one generation instead of four. God, I'm so tired I'm repeating this stuff like a parrot from Orthis' own words. What you do, of course, is alter the germ plasm of both parents before conception takes place, and . . . anyway, it's all here."

Quorn said suddenly, "This place looks as good as any. At least it'll give us a little more cover."

He took the skiff down carefully toward the flat bed of an ancient watercourse. The channel was filled now with frozen air, but in bygone ages it had gouged a deep canyon in the rock, leaving eroded holes and overhangs. Quorn worked the skiff into one of these washed-out places, under the canyon wall.

Edri was going over his book again, making sure, dazed with the hypnosis of exhaustion and the need to be right. He did not dare to fumble or read a single figure wrong. There wouldn't be any time for corrections or recheckings. The weight of the responsibility was so heavy on him that he seemed to be physically shrinking under it. His lips moved constantly. Trehearne did not envy him his job.

Quorn grunted at him and they went aft together to struggle with the ultra-wave equipment. Trehearne was possessed by a demon of urgency, and he had not the slightest idea what he was doing. Quorn gave orders and he obeyed them blindly, sometimes right, sometimes wrong. Nerve and temper were worn to the last frayed edge and beyond, and before they were through they were snarling at each other like dogs. Hooking the power leads to the skiff's generators was the hardest task of all, but somehow they finished. They lifted Edri to his feet and sat him down again, still clutching his book, in front of the transmitter. Quorn bent over the control switches. The generators hummed, feeding in the power. Edri was still staring at the book. Trehearne shook him. "Go on," he said. "Talk."

Edri blinked and frowned, looking up at them as though he had forgotten entirely what he had to do. Quorn took Edri's face between his hands and spoke to him, slapping his cheeks gently one after the other as he talked. "Listen, I've got it on the emergency band, covering all channels. Every ultra-wave receiver within its range will pick it up, including non-Vardda communication centers. Edri, do you understand me? The minute Kerrel picks it up he'll be able to center us and come in on our beam. So you've got to make it fast. Fast!"

Edri blinked again, and shivered. "All right. I'll try." He glanced nervously at Trehearne. Quorn made the last dial setting, and then he spoke into the transmitter.

"G-One! G-One! Emergency. Request clearance all channels. Use your recorders! Use your recorders! G-One, clear all channels . . ."

He motioned violently, and Edri leaned forward. "I may not have time to repeat. We have found the ship of Orthis. Here follow the formulae for the Vardda mutation."

XXI

EDRI HAD BEGUN TO READ FROM THE NOTEBOOK. HE was going fast, but taking desparate pains to make each syllable clear. Quorn hung tensely over his dial. Trehearne sat motionless, except that his muscles quivered. Sweat ran in his eyes. He was tired. He was so tired that Quorn, three feet away, looked as blurred and indistinct as though he were lost in the haze of distance. Edri's voice went on, and on, and on.

Quorn said hoarsely, "The cruiser has picked us up. They're already trying to jam us. Hurry up."

Edri's face became that of a hunted thing. His voice rose shrill, racing desperately. He turned the last page. He finished it, and then he went back to the beginning and started to repeat. Quorn stood up.

"It isn't any use, we're blanked out. That means the cruiser's close, close enough to . . ."

He didn't have time to get the rest of the words out. The skiff was shaken suddenly as by a giant hand. Quorn was flung against a bulkhead, and Trehearne lay on the floor. Only Edri, hanging on to the transmitter, still talked.

"Shell burst," Quorn said, getting up again. "They're ranging us down the canyon." He reached for his helmet. The skiff shuddered a second time, harder. Trehearne scrambled painfully to his feet. He tried to jam Edri's helmet down over his head, but Edri fought him, clinging to the transmitter. Quorn laid hold of him and yelled, "You're not getting through any more! Come on!" He closed the master switch. Between them they got Edri's hands loose and the helmet on him. The skiff was racked again, and something broke with a crackle of exploding glass. Trehearne locked his own helmet. Through the audio he could hear Quorn shouting something about the airlock and getting clear before the skiff was blasted flat with them inside it. Half dragging Edri between them, they began to run. Some of the deck plates were already buckled, and there was an ominous shrill whistle of escaping air. They reached the lock and got it open.

Out on the canyon floor a great light blossomed and died. Chunks of rock struck silently against the skiff. The deck leaped under their feet, and the airlock spewed them out as the hull rocked over. They hit the ground hard, too hard. For the space of several seconds they lay where they were, and there were no more shell bursts. Trehearne groaned and sat up. "I guess that was the last one. Quorn? Edri? Somebody answer me."

Edri was silent, but Quorn said thickly, "They know we quit sending. Damn it, I've cut my mouth on the helmet rim and it's bleeding all over me." Trehearne could hear him spitting. He crawled over and shook Edri. Presently Edri said, "Where's the notebook?"

"Still in the skiff."

"We've got to get it . . ."

"What for?"

"I guess you're right. Did we do it, Quorn? Did we put it through?"

"I don't know, I don't know! They came in on us so fast . . ."

He got up off the ground, looking at something, and then he pointed, up into the black sky. "Are we going to run," he asked, "or wait?"

Trehearne looked up and down the river bed that was clogged with air, frozen, and then along the cruel, cold line of the cliffs above. "We could breathe for a few hours, all right, till our oxygen gave out. But it hardly seems worth it."

Quorn sat down again. "I guess we wait."

They waited, and the cruiser dropped down silently

151

out of the sky. It was dark in the canyon, where the cliffs cut off the galactic light, but the cruiser's ports shone brightly. Trehearne was almost glad to see them. They were human. They were comforting, after all the night and desolation of a dead world. The airlock opened and a vivid shaft of brilliance shot out of it, going straight on with no air to diffuse it, until it hit the opposite wall of the canyon, near the skiff. Men in pressure suits began to come out of the lock. Trehearne rose. He stepped into the bright beam and walked slowly toward the men. Edri came after him, and Quorn.

A voice he did not know spoke over the helmet phone. "Identify yourselves."

They gave their names, and Trehearne added, "We're unarmed. We're through." There was a certain relief in being through. Whatever happened from here on was out of their hands. They could sit passively and rest, and let it happen. He looked at the ship and thought of warmth and light and food and comfort, and most of all he thought of sleep. Shairn and Kerrel could come later.

The men from the cruiser carried weapons, a type of shock-rifle more deadly than the little tubes that only stunned. They came out a short distance, toward the three bulky shapes that shuffled down the beam of light. The first voice that had spoken gave an order, and the two men went off toward the skiff to search it, their belt lamps bobbing. Then it spoke again to Trehearne and the others. "Keep your hands as high as you can. All right, that's far enough."

Trehearne said, "I told you, we're unarmed."

"Precaution. Stand where you are."

They stood, and were searched.

"Very well," said the officer's voice. "Come aboard."

"No."

One short word, spoken quietly in a voice that Trehearne knew. A voice he had not heard for a long, long time, but that he remembered. Kerrel's voice. Some of the exhaustion in him stirred and drew back, and anger took his place. The men stood in the beam of light, but with their backs toward it, facing their prisoners. The undiffused glare passed around them, leaving their faces in darkness, invisible behind the helmet plates. Trehearne tried to identify Kerrel, but he could not.

The officer said, rather irritably, "But there's no point in standing out here any longer." The case had been long and hard for him, too. "We take off as soon as the search detail comes back."

"Yes," said Kerrel. "But not them. They stay here."

The suited shapes, the faceless and unhuman shapes that had stood together drew apart a little and turned toward each other, as though they tried to pierce the darkness with their peering helmet plates. There was a silence of astonishment, and then Edri said, "That's murder."

The voice of the officer, rising on a note of anger, demanded, "Kerrel, what the hell— Have you gone clean crazy?"

"Is justice a crazy thing?" There was something strange about Kerrel's voice. It was flat and toneless and devoid of passion, the voice of a man with too much inside himself to bear, too much to find escape through any normal channels. "They may have succeeded. Do you understand that? They may, just possibly, have done what they set out to do. Do you know what that would mean?"

"As well as you do. And don't worry about justice, they'll get it. But they'll get it from the Council on Llyrdis, according to law."

"Law," said Kerrel softly. "Once Trehearne received the benefit of our law. I told them then that they were wrong to give it to him. The law is good, I've served it all my life. But there are times when one has to go beyond the law if one is to go on serving it. Leave them here."

Trehearne spoke, for the first time. "It wouldn't do for me to go back to Llyrdis, would it, Kerrel? Not to stand up in open Council and tell exactly how and why Yann died."

Kerrel's voice answered him, and he could not tell which of the helmeted shapes was speaking, the shapes with the shadowed faces. It was maddening not to know.

"And was I wrong, Trehearne? Could you stand up in open Council and say that I was wrong to try it?"

"Listen," said the officer. "I'm not judge and I'm not jury. I was sent out by the Council to bring these men in, and I'm going to do it. For God's sake, Kerrel, stop trying to carry the weight of the universe on your shoulders. No man is that big. Come on, you three—into the ship."

"No."

One figure detached itself. One figure drew away from the rest of the group and stood between them and the ship, with a shock-rifle in its hands.

"You're not thinking far enough ahead. Suppose they've failed. Should they be put on trial—under a law and a system that they've risked their lives to tear down —should they be allowed to talk to the whole galaxy about what they've done, to become heroes and martyrs, a focal point of trouble for all time to come?"

"There have been Orthist trials before." The officer was moving toward Kerrel. "I think you'd better give me that rifle, before you get carried away."

The muzzle of the shock-gun lifted, and Kerrel said, "Wait, I'm not finished yet." The officer took another step and then he hesitated, and an uneasiness seemed to come over him and the rest of the cruiser's men. Trehearne's belly contracted with a sick impotent fury and his hands moved forward in a grasping motion, futile, hungry. Quorn was cursing in a monotone, so low that it only formed a background for the voices speaking over it.

Kerrel said, "These men are different. They found the ship, the shrine. They've been inside it, handled the notebooks, for all I know they've seen the body of Orthis himself. They proved it could be done. Will that ever be forgotten?"

"I don't give a damn," the officer said. "No one is going to kill prisoners. Give me the gun."

Kerrel stepped back, just a little, a step or two. The group of men began to widen out, slowly, leaving one by one the beam of light until only three were left, a small screen between Kerrel and the prisoners. Trehearne's legs bent and flexed. He watched the gun.

Kerrel said, "Suppose they didn't fail. Suppose it's all over, the thousand years of Vardda life. Should they be allowed to enjoy the thing they've done?"

"Fine talk," Trehearne said. The darkness was deep and close, outside the beam. "Noble talk. Maybe I even believe it. But you've got another reason, too."

154

"I admit it. But in this, it doesn't matter. No woman ever born was important enough to matter in this." He asked quietly of the officer, "Will you leave them here?"

"Will you put that gun down!"

Back another step. "You three men there, in front of the prisoners. Move aside."

"All right," said the officer. *"Jump him!"*

Trehearne sprang for the darkness. He saw the three men in front of him melt away. The rifle cracked and flared, not aimed at anyone just yet, a warning. And then the night was full of motion.

Lying on the black rock. on the iron ridges of frozen air that flowed between, Trehearne watched the clumsy dance of men in shapeless pressure suits and round blank helmets, in and out of the sharp bright beam that was empty now except for themselves. They had moved around Kerrel in the blackness and the silence and come upon him from the back, but their hands were hampered by the gauntlets and the bulging fabric of Kerrel's suit was hard to hold. They lost him, and then he was part of the group again and they did not know which one, and their voices rose in an angry babble. Only Kerrel did not speak. Trehearne crept on his belly, farther away from the beam, and the shadows that were Quorn and Edri followed him. Suddenly Edri tapped his helmet, and then pointed, and Trehearne saw the solitary figure of a man walking in the darkness outside the beam, but from this angle showing black against it, toward the place where the prisoners had been.

Trehearne said aloud, "This is Trehearne speaking. He's coming our way, to your right and just outside the beam."

The men began to run, spreading out. And then the shock-rifle flared and flared again, steady, systematic, raking all the ground where the prisoners should be, the blue bolts cracking in the helmet phones like heavy static. Trehearne and the others fled farther away, floundering over the bitter ground, and the blue bolts haunted them, and then two men flung themselves at Kerrel from behind. He fell, dropping the rifle.

The two men got up after a moment, rather slowly. Someone came with a belt lamp, and then others, and then all of them, with Trehearne and Quorn and Edri.

They all stood looking down at the figure that still lay where it had fallen and did not move. There was a ridge of rock with sharp teeth edging it, sticking up from the frozen air.

"He hit hard," said one of the men, "right on his face-plate, and it broke."

The officer swore, viciously. "What a stinking mess! Why did he have to do it? He must have been crazy."

"I don't know," Trehearne said slowly. "Where do you draw the line between lunacy and belief? If there'd been more like him, we couldn't have done what we did."

They picked Kerrel up and carried him to the cruiser, and Trehearne plodded on where he was told. Inside the ship he and the others were stripped of their pressure suits and searched again for weapons. Then guards took them down a corridor, tired bitter men who had been too long on a grinding job. One of them said, "We over-hauled the *Mirzim*. All your friends are here." And then he added, "It's a pity that we have to save the lives of men like you."

They came to a heavy door and stopped, and Shairn was standing there. She looked thin, and her eyes were shadowed, and there were lines around her mouth that had not been there before. She was not the old Shairn. She was someone new. There was no joy in that meeting. She looked at Trehearne and said, "Michael, what have you done?"

He shook his head and answered, "That's the hell of it. We may not have done anything at all."

XXII

THE VOYAGE WAS ENDING. THEY HAD KNOWN FROM THE long period of deceleration that it was ending, and now the last pressures, and the small, grinding shocks as the cruiser settled into its dock, told them that they were again on Llyrdis. The bells rang, and the throb of the generators gave way to an unfamiliar silence.

They waited, then. And nothing happened. The hours went by and nothing happened.

Trehearne said finally, "They're not even going to remove us from the cruiser. They'll take us off to wherever we're bound for without even hearing us."

Edri shook his head. "No. Vardda law sentences no man without formal trial."

They could see nothing, hear nothing. Until, at last, the door was unlocked. There were officers and guards —many guards, all of them armed. Their faces told nothing.

"You will come with us," said the young captain of guards soberly.

"Where?" demanded Joris. "To Llyrdis prison or—"

"All communication with the prisoners forbidden," clipped the young captain. "You will come with us."

It seemed strange to Trehearne to walk again on unmoving floors, corridors, decks—on a planet. The tawny glare of Aldebaran was dazzling when they filed out of the cruiser. The air seemed unnaturally damp, heavy with the tang of the sea.

He and Joris and Edri, the first to emerge, looked around with a throb of eagerness, of half-hope. They could not see much. The cruiser had landed in a closed-off sector and there were other guards waiting out here beside a number of the sleek cars.

But Trehearne could hear. He could hear all the usual hum and din and clangor of the vast spaceport, the grind of cranes and rumble of trams, the scream of a fast planet-flyer coming in. And then the *whoosh* of a great bulk hurtling upward, a star-ship outbound for distant suns. And in the distance the shining towers of Llyrdis city still magnificently challenged the heavens.

Trehearne felt a sick sense of futility. All this vast ordered turmoil of routine and activity, all the galaxy-wide trade that centered here, the thousand-year solidity of Vardda commercial monopoly—how could he have dreamed that a pitifully faint and aborted radio call could ever shake it? The faces of his friends showed him how their last hope had begun to wane.

"The cars," said the young captain. "You four will go in the first one."

Edri found his voice. "What about Arrin?"

"I am permitted to tell you that your comrade has been removed to hospital and is in good conditon."

Joris said nothing. Trehearne saw his sunken eyes looking across the spaceport and thought how it must be for him to come back thus to this place where for years he had sat with his hands guiding the Vardda ships that came and went. Then the car took them out of the spaceport, fast. Trehearne saw that other cars, with guards alone in them, ran unobtrusively along ahead of and behind them.

And nothing was changed in Llyrdis. The peacock city preened itself beneath the sun, iridescent, splendid, its streets thronged with the smiling Vardda and the other stranger races—echoing with music, brilliant with color. They passed a Vardda man and girl who stood, laughing as they talked. And it was then that Trehearne ceased altogether to hope.

"We're going to the Council Hall," Edri said presently.

Joris nodded somberly. "I could have told you that. As a Council member, I have to be formally impeached and removed before charges against me can be pressed." He added grimly, "Old Ristin, the chairman, won't weep over that. We tangled pretty often, in the past."

The Council Hall sat amid a crowded nexus of governmental buildings. It dominated Llyrdis, not by size, but by age. It was a grey old pile, without beauty but with the massiveness and solidity of eternal things. Its courts and corridors and staring officials Trehearne saw only vaguely. They slid over his vision, and nothing seemed entirely tangible until, in an anteroom, Shairn's face leaped real to his eyes.

She had been waiting to see him pass, he knew. Her face was white and strained, and she said nothing, but her eyes said, *"Michael! Michael!"* He looked back at her as they went on and he wondered what she read in his own eyes. And then they had entered the deliberative chamber itself.

It was not large and not crowded, a half-moon-shaped hall with something more than a hundred Vardda in its chairs. Of the blur of faces turned toward him, most were grave, some curious, some open in their hatred.

Ristin, the chairman, was a magnificent white-haired old Lucifer who disdained the petty vanity of pretending that this was a routine matter.

"This Council is not a judicial body," he informed the four. "The criminal charges against you—piracy, resisting of authority—will be handled by the regular courts. We are here investigating a matter urgent to the state."

Joris got up, thrusting his grey head forward like an old mastiff's. He growled, "Since this is an investigation, you can't legally carry it out without hearing us."

Ristin said grimly, "The Coordinator of the Port was always good at making himself heard here. But you will have to wait this time, Joris." He looked up at the watching Vardda faces as he added, "The problem of your personal offense is not foremost. What concerns us most urgently is the general policy to be adopted by the Council."

Trehearne hardly heard. That glimpse of Shairn had done things to him and his mind was far away. He wondered vaguely why Edri, who had sat sagging heavily beside him, suddenly stiffened, why Edri convulsively grasped his wrist.

Ristin was continuing, "Therefore I emphasize again that we of the Council must not let any emotion of resentment sway our judgment. We are elected to serve the best interests of the Vardda as a whole and we must let no lesser considerations in any way affect our decision."

Then Joris laughed. His head came up, and his bellowing laughter echoed and re-echoed from the vaulted roof. He swung around to Trehearne and Edri and Quorn, and his eyes were blazing now. *"By God, you did it after all!"*

Trehearne, still only half understanding, felt a white-hot thrill. Edri had begun to tremble violently.

Ristin's cool voice cut in. "Believe me, your exulatation is premature. Nevertheless there is no purpose in concealing the fact that your actions have presented us with an unprecedentedly grave problem."

Quorn said hoarsely to Trehearne, "Don't you get it? Our message got through!"

Trehearne understood then. The gravity of the watching faces, the bitter hatred in some of them, the strong leadership the old chairman was wielding to conquer the crisis—all these belied the everyday appearance of Llyrdis that had been the death-knell of his hopes. He knew, now. He knew that through them, after a thousand years, the voice of Orthis had spoken to the Galaxy. And it had been heard—somewhere it had been heard.

Ristin was saying, "So far only vague rumor and hearsay is abroad. Every operator who might have heard the broadcast has been warned not to repeat it but there are bound to be Orthists among them. The fact that non-Vardda worlds possess ultra-wave receivers for use in their commerce with us is an even more serious matter. It stands thus—that in spite of the news-services' cooperation with us on the matter, it is slowly becoming public knowledge that Orthis' secret was found and broadcast. At least three recordings of it have been found, and two written records. We can assume that there are more."

Joris said grimly, "In other words—the secret is out and everyone will soon know that—and what are you going to do about it?"

"The Coordinator of the Port has summed it up," Ristin agreed, coolly. "What shall we do about it?"

A tall Vardda leaped up and cried, "I suggest that the first thing we do is to execute these traitors!"

There was a fierce chorus of agreement from a few dozen voices. Ristin called sharply for order.

"I have reminded you that our paramount consideration at this moment must be the ultimate best interests of our people! Let us have no more such outbreaks."

An older Vardda man rose in the tiers and said quietly, "Before I advance my suggestion I should admit that I have always had secret Orthist sympathies. I don't think that I am the only one here who can say that. You must allow for that." He went on. "I would have liked long ago to see this unnatural monopoly ended. Now our hand has been forced. I suggest that our best and wisest course is to act at once—to declare publicly that we Vardda are going to *give* the secret to the whole Galaxy."

He paused, to emphasize his point. "The secret is out anyway. But by acting quickly we can take credit for that. We can aver that the broadcast was made with our consent. Remember, whether we like it or not, in a few generations other worlds will be flying the stars—and we do not want them cherishing a legacy of hatred for us then."

Trehearne, listening, smiled grimly. "Politics don't change much across the galaxy."

"But it's all we hoped for," Edri whispered. "It would work, too!"

Discussion, angry debate, had sprung up. It went on and on, passionate voices accusing and denying, Ristin sternly maintaining order, bringing back the argument to the main issue time after time. Finally, in a lull of the disputing voices, Joris swung around and faced the Council.

"Now listen to me," the old man roared. "You'd think the way some of you talk that this meant the end of the Vardda, the end of Llyrdis, the end of everything. That's utter asininity. In the first place, mutations don't take place overnight. It will be a generation or two before the other races start going out between the stars in any numbers."

Trehearne saw that sink home. The Vardda Council,

161

being human, could not worry too deeply for long about a future they wouldn't see.

"And furthermore," Joris bellowed, "when every half-baked folk in the galaxy does take to starflight, does that mean the great Vardda trade is ruined forever? Listen! We Vardda were the first to go out to the stars. *The first!* Do you think all the lubberly races of the galaxy can compete with us out there? Do you think so?"

He caught them with that, with the Vardda pride, the Vardda glory. Trehearne saw the strained faces changing. Not all of them, but many.

Joris paused before he said his final word. "Do you think there will ever be a time when we Vardda can't hold our own?"

There was not much talk after that. There were questions, protests, doubts, but little more argument. All the arguments had been spoken.

"We have to decide this now or never," Ristin told them. "If we delay longer, there will not be a choice."

Trehearne heard the resolution read, and the voting and the result. Not easily could the Vardda yield! Forty-three voted against the resolution. But seventy-nine for it.

Ristin said, "It will be announced by general broadcast tonight that, in view of the advance of civilization on many star-worlds, the Vardda deem the time ripe to share the secret of mutation with other selected races."

Quorn said, "It's done. Trehearne, it's done."

Trehearne still could not quite grasp that that simple statement marked a change forever in the galaxy, that with it all human races began the great change toward Galactic Man.

"And these criminals who forced us to do the thing?" demanded a Vardda recalcitrant, glaring at Trehearne and his fellows.

"We have no choice there," Ristin said dryly. "To punish them for what they did would belie our own announcement. The ordinary charges against them can be dismissed."

"So that for their crime they go unpunished?"

Ristin sighed regretfully. "The interests of the state demand it. Yes."

Trehearne's comrades were breaking down, half stunned, half incredulous of the victory they had thought beyond them. But strangely Trehearne was not thinking of what they had won for the galactic races. He was feeling a pride that Joris' phrase, "We Vardda," had kindled in him.

"We Vardda—"

And he was one of them. He was one of the star-lords, the first, the oldest, the greatest of the starmen.

Edri was thinking of something else. He had stepped forward amid the general clamor to speak to Ristin. "There is one more thing. Orthis—"

"A cruiser has been sent to guard his ship," said Ristin.

Edri nodded painfully. "But Orthis was not ever child of a planet. He was star-born, dwelling always between the stars. He has sat long on that far world. If his ship could take space again . . ."

Ristin said musingly, "A good thought. By putting that ship into an orbit around our system we'll create a monument that will remind all the galaxy that it was a Vardda who gave them star-flight."

Edri turned to Trehearne and Joris. He had tears in his eyes. He said, "Orthis is going home."

The message left for Trehearne had told him simply that Shairn would be at the Silver Tower. It was handed him when they finally emerged from the Council Hall. Joris got him a car and driver. Trehearne hesitated, suddenly hating to part from the old man. Edri, and Quorn and the others had their eager plans. But Joris took no joy in their victory.

"Had it been done a generation ago my son would be a star-captain now," he muttered, in answer to Trehearne's awkward words. "Well—"

The car took him out of the city, smooth and fast, and the great flare of Aldebaran sank toward the sea and dusk came on. The stars burgeoned and Trehearne looked up at them. He looked at the far faint spark of little Sol, and thought of Earth and of a changeling born there who had by a miracle won his way home.

That green and distant Earth knew nothing yet of the battle fought and won beyond the edges of the galaxy.

163

But it had been Earth's battle too and she would know of it in time. Even to Earth, when a generation had passed, the star-ships would begin to go openly. And with their internecine conflicts past, Earth's young men too would go out among the stars to join the great march of Galactic Man. Who could say where that march might not lead them? To other galaxies, other island continents of suns . . .

Trehearne's thoughts came back from the immensities of the future when he saw the Silver Tower glimmering in the starlight. He left the car and walked toward it, and then he saw the pale figure on the shadowy beach beside the slow wash of the sea, and he went down to it.

He put out his arms to her, but she held him off. She spoke to him, her voice clear, her face a white blur in the darkness. "I won't have hidden things between us, Michael. I want you to know. I hate you for what you've done to the Vardda. I'll always hate you for it."

He stepped back and let his arms fall. "In that case," he said, "I'd better go."

"No, wait." She came to him and put her hands on either side of his face, very gently, and she said, "I love you, in spite of everything. I don't know why. My mind keeps telling me all the reasons why I shouldn't, but— it's a queer thing, Michael. I've never been in love before. Will you have me on those grounds?"

He held her this time, tight against him, and his lips brushed over hers as he answered, "Life with you won't be any haven of peace, I'm sure. But I knew that when I found you."

Standing with her in the gloom, the sea-wind rumpling her white robe and tumbling her hair, memory tricked him back to that night on the Breton beach, centuries ago. So far and far he had come since then, and yet of it all that was almost his clearest memory.

He knew now, with a wisdom that he had not had before, that it would always be so with a man—that it was not the conflicts and the pain and the triumph, not the empires and the stars and the struggles that the memory clung to the longest. It was the little things, the sound of a girl's laughter, the cry of birds on the sea-wind, the flare of a long-ago sunset, that a man held, that he would always hold, when everything else was gone.

ABOUT THE AUTHOR

Leigh Brackett began her outstanding career in science fiction in 1940 when her "Martian Quest" was published in *Astounding*. She was best known for her heroic adventures featuring larger-than-life swashbucklers such as Eric John Stark—her most famous character and hero of *The Book of Skaith*. In addition to sf, Leigh Brackett acquired a long list of screenplay credits at major Hollywood studios. Her first screen assignment was a collaboration with William Faulkner on the screen adapation of *The Big Sleep*.

Just before her untimely death in 1978, she completed the first draft of the screenplay of *The Empire Strikes Back*, the sequel to *Star Wars*.